PRAISE FOR NO CALL TOO SMALL

"Martens's striking, perceptive collection illuminates a range of Canadians in moments of bad luck and dissatisfaction. In the title story, an unnamed Port Moody, B.C., cop, whose face has been disfigured from a dog attack, refuses to wear his prosthetic nose, costing him his relationship and earning him the nickname "The Face." Martens's haunting, darkly funny situations, captured in crisp, spare prose, will appeal to fans of George Saunders."

— *Publishers Weekly*

"Oscar Martens's characters hurtle their way toward potential disaster or redemption in these vivid stories of lives burdened by misunderstandings and disappointment, usually self-inflicted. Martens's strong prose is a pleasure to read, with dark humour and lively storytelling that brings a quirky humanity to his characters."

— Janie Chang, author of *Dragon Springs Road*

"A young girl stuck on a Ferris wheel in a lightning storm, caught between the madness of her manic, idiot father and a withdrawn mother. A group of locals watching the action as a boat launch becomes a dangerous, bitterly complex, and life defining moment. A young man following his heart in a car that is barely alive – a car held together by desire and temerity. A dystopian nightmare that flips the world upside-down and inside-out. Oscar Martens is the twitchy love child of Tom Waits, Charles Bukowski and Ricky Gervais. These stories are lean, and loaded, and devastatingly true. In just a few pages, Martens throws his readers into the deep end of a swimming pool swarming with sharks, or piranhas, or hungry polar bears—and you, dear reader, have a flesh wound. These short stories read like brilliant, poignant novels. Highly recommended."

— Thomas Trofimuk, author of *Waiting for Columbus*

"Oscar Martens's collection is a warm, safe port in the storm that is life these days. His writing is vivid and clear, his characters honest and their stories full of the details and emotional truth that make them real. I read these stories, one by one, as a nightly ritual, as a special treat before going to sleep to call up the dreams that make for a peaceful sleep."

— Jennifer Haupt, Editor, *One True Thing, Psychology Today*

NO
CALL
TOO
SMALL

STORIES

OSCAR MARTENS

central
avenue
publishing

Published by Central Avenue Publishing, an imprint of Central Avenue Marketing Ltd.
www.centralavenuepublishing.com

Published in Canada

Printed in United States of America

1. FICTION / Short Stories - Single Author   2. FICTION / Literary

Library and Archives Canada Cataloguing in Publication

Title: No call too small : stories / Oscar Martens.

Names: Martens, Oscar, 1968- author.

Identifiers: Canadiana (print) 2020015902X | Canadiana (ebook) 20200159038 | ISBN 9781771681957

(softcover) | ISBN 9781771681964 (HTML) | ISBN 9781771681971 (Kindle)

Classification: LCC PS8576.A7654 N62 2020 | DDC C813/.6—dc23

10 9 8 7 6 5 4 3 2 1

For Lyette

CONTENTS

NO
CALL
TOO
SMALL

NO CALL TOO SMALL

WE SIT IN OUR CRUISER AT THE FAR END of the lot in Belcarra Park, where all is calm except for the two squirrels I've been tracking. Observed but unreported, one has scored a cheese doodle from under the picnic bench, and the other seems determined to take it by force, spiralling up the trunk of a nearby pine. Subject is a few inches tall; half a pound; light-brown fur; bushy tail; nervous, darting eyes; and twitchy body language. Victim is a few inches tall; half a pound; light-brown fur; bushy tail; nervous, darting eyes; and twitchy body language. The sharp crack that startles me is not gunfire, but a seagull dropping a clam onto the pavement to smash open its shell. This seagull of interest is known to police and has been seen in the area with his associates, harassing the eagle that now sits atop an eighty-foot cedar. Current rainy conditions do not warrant intervention.

The long road in creates a secluded feeling, with evergreens crowding in so tightly that the sun rarely dries out the green trail of slime running down the centre of the lanes. Down on the dock, anglers keep their small-fry catch in pails. Theft, though not likely, is possible. We monitor this entire park, from the barbeques to the gazebos, down to the beach where kids overturn rocks to watch crabs scatter. These are the mean streets of Port Moody, now peaceful, but only until rival families clash over the last shaded picnic table. Angelo takes a sip of his coffee and stares out over the water before asking my opinion.

—Do you think Rockford was happy?

I know he's referring to Jim Rockford of *The Rockford Files*, a popular show from the '70s about a private investigator.

—Single guy. Lives in a trailer. Does that sound happy?

—But it's waterfront, and he can move that trailer any time.

Rockford doesn't carry a gun. It isn't, as Angelo assumes, a spiritual angle, a belief that the world can be negotiated without force, or a Buddhist-inspired pledge to non-violence, or the triumph of intelligence over thuggery. It's because Rockford is a felon. Angelo won't hear this, because that's not the Rockford he knows and loves. He romanticizes a life I see as quiet, hard, and lonely. Rockford may have an ocean view, but the trailer stigma never dies, no matter where you park it. Imagine his date stepping inside, clutching her purse a little tighter, hoping that when her eyes adjust to the darkness, her grim expectations will be proven wrong. Can you call it a home if someone can tow it in fifteen minutes? At night, rats lured to the food stands sniff out scattered crumbs from hot-dog buns and french fries dropped in the sand. They can easily chew through the cheap flooring in the trailer if there aren't already plenty of cracks and holes.

Without the most basic barriers, the trailer is vulnerable to attack. There's no fence or hedge to slow down an approach, should anyone wish to hurt him, and plenty would. A large truck could level his "home" in seconds. Rockford is not really there. There is no post, beam, or foundation that fixes his structure to the ground. He has no current or future claim on that corner of the parking lot. No one in the area considers him a neighbour or would fight for his right to be there. His stay depends on the indifference or generosity of local authorities. What kind of life is that? Angelo won't acknowledge the difference between living in a waterfront house and squatting in a prefab shack. Our bum PI is borrowing his seaside experience, not owning it.

Angelo resembles Rockford if Rockford were a young, trim, good-looking Italian. His light build and courteous manner suggest he's ill-equipped to tackle a drunken hooligan, but that never seems necessary. Calm tones prevail on our shift, and Angelo would likely be talking about last night's game by the time he tucked a wild one into the backseat of our car. He drove me to this park during our first patrol together, and I was surprised to find this much wilderness on the edge of Port Moody. I'd been through Stanley Park and up North Shore mountains, but Belcarra is a low-traffic area, off the major routes, and that day, we almost had it to ourselves. When we came to the end of the parking lot, he stopped the car and turned to me.

—Would you mind if I looked at your face for a few minutes? I only have to do this once.

He stared at the hole where my nose used to be, the wound left by the dog's teeth, lingering on the main show for half a minute before moving on to the deep scars on my cheeks and the small, triangular cutout on my upper lip where teeth show even when I'm not smiling. Angelo leaned closer, drawn into my topography, a terrain of pathways, lines, and trenches.

—I think your face is leaking.

Clair said almost the same thing after I told her there would be no more surgeries. Frankenface was tired of the cutting and the stitching and the sculpting and the shaping. She brought my prosthetic and a box of Kleenex from the bathroom and slammed them down in front of me. The clip-on was supposed to boost my self-esteem, but the past cannot be restored like an antique chair.

—Why don't you wear your nose?

—It's a prosthetic.

—It's a nose. It's 95 percent better than having no nose.

—It's 100 percent fake.

Do you like me better in disguise? Do you like this better than the truth? I considered, then aborted, a dozen things I could say to slow her progress through the house. I sat at the dinner table, rolling the blob of silicone between my palms, wondering if the colour could be adjusted with makeup to match my skin tone as we cycled through the seasons. She often used her overnight bag whenever she stomped over to her sister's place, the final punctuation to any fight, but that night I heard the bumping and scraping of the big hard suitcase she hauled from the back of the closet. She paused to let me know she had no choice but to distance herself from someone she considered self-destructive. She wouldn't watch while I did this to myself.

I never had the chance to tell her about the Whittaker rape at

Suter Brook Towers the week before, how I got into the back of the car with that kid who had been wisely silent up to that point, how I faced him, secretly pleased with his horror, asking simple questions as the member in the front seat scrambled to write it all down. On Thursday, a young hothead with bloody knuckles and a blind fury for anything in punching range just stopped, straightened up from his fighting stance, and stared at me, long enough for the bruised bouncer to get him in a headlock.

When it's time to roll out of the park and stop some crime, I open the window to take in the forest air, as I always do. Tiny Tim, my first partner, would always whine and complain when I did this, turning the heat up to maximum. Tiny was just like Harry Callahan in the *Dirty Harry* movies minus the driving, shooting, squinting, punching, and crime solving. Every one of Tiny's 280 pounds was unhappy to be stuck with The Face, and I wasn't thrilled to be paired with a guy who seemed determined to take on life from a seated position. How typical that one so desperately in need of exercise would do anything to avoid it, insisting on drive-through, assuring me at every traffic stop that he'd get the next one.

—Do you think someone could actually pull off the fire-hose stunt?

Angelo is driving very slowly, as if he too is straining to consider all the possibilities posed by his own question. In the first *Die Hard* movie, John McClane is on the roof of an office tower that has been rigged with explosives by a bunch of foreign terrorists. John stands at the edge of the roof, understandably hesitant, when a helicopter with a sniper hovers into view. John more or less drops off the edge as the roof explodes, but when he hits the side of the building, he doesn't break through the glass. He's forced to plant his bloody feet against the window, spring off, and shoot his way through, landing roughly on a pile of shards.

Angelo points to the rusted-out Corolla on the side of the road with its right headlight smashed.

—Isn't that Clement's car?

He's half off the road, the underside of the car hung up on the shoulder. Angelo sees the bright patch of colour in the ditch before I do, a cyclist next to his mangled bike, not moving. We get out and find Clement still in the driver's seat, seemingly unable to form words, a nice little pile of puke in his lap, some painted over the steering wheel. Angelo reaches down to the floor of the car, pulls out the half-full bottle of vodka, and throws it into the bush, lazy arcs of booze spitting from the mouth like a wonky sprinkler. He wants me to use the cruiser to nudge Clement's car back onto the road.

—What about the guy in the ditch?

—He's gone, Face. Look at the angle of his neck.

I go over and check anyway, my warm fingers on his cold, wet wrist. It looks like he was launched into the ditch headfirst, the weight of his body snapping his neck.

—Let's go, Face! Running out of time here.

I look up from the bright, spandex-wrapped corpse as my partner loads Clement into the backseat of the Corolla. I can't move, or won't, staring at Angelo as the cold rain works its way down the back of my neck.

—Am I doing this by myself?

Still not moving, not talking. I hope another car comes along, or a school bus with twenty sets of unblinking eyes to witness this, even a single person, walking her dog along the side of the road. Looking up into the clouds, drops sting my eyes with tiny shocks. Somehow, somewhere, in that grey, stewing mass, vapour bonds with dust, and droplets are born, joining into heavier drops that blow apart when they hit the hood of the car. The fragments are reabsorbed into a blob, and when the mass overwhelms surface tension, it bursts into a rivulet, a tiny vein-like stream that joins others as they flow down the slope toward the ground.

—Face!

Nobody's a criminal yet. Nobody's a liar. Maybe if we stand still we can maintain this pure state, three cops holding rigid against the future. A crow scolds vigorously from a nearby tree as Angelo uses the cruiser to push on Clement's car. He switches over to the Corolla and floors it, the wheels spitting out bits of gravel and grass as it pulls off the shoulder, and then they're gone, blue smoke hanging in the air.

The crime scene is more complicated now: chips off the Corolla's taillight shattered by Angelo as he pushed; glass from the right front headlight at the point of impact; the long, angry trail of the spinning tire. I see this area cordoned off with yellow tape, the entrance to the park closed to incoming traffic, a poster with nicely labelled photos on an easel in a courtroom, evidence markers like yellow flowers growing from the pavement, counting off a series of mistakes. And the bottle, with its excellent prints, still in the bush, where no one will look for it.

I spit out water that has funneled into my wound, and my thoughts return to the bruised and bloody John McClane, standing at the edge of the roof. There's plenty to consider before he jumps. Assuming a fifty-foot drop, he might be close to half of terminal velocity by the time it came tight. The hose has little flexibility, so the stress at the point of attachment would be significant. It could easily snap his back. If it were tied around his waist, it might spin him like a propeller, sending his gun flying. Also, how much does a cop know about tying knots? If he ties a bowline, the loop won't tighten on him, but he might slip through. If the knot slips, it will cinch tight on his body at the end of the drop, breaking his ribs, or clamping down so hard on his chest that he won't be able to breathe. John stands on the edge, the odd gust pulling at his pant legs while he considers two equally unappealing choices.

The biker sucks in a huge, jagged breath and rolls over onto his back. His eyes follow mine until they don't. While I call for an ambulance, there are two shallow breaths and nothing more. It's impossible to get directly over his chest on the muddy slope, so I push on an angle instead of straight down, afraid that a shift might damage his neck. My muscles already burn, and I can't even hear the sirens yet. Bright blood streams out of his nose, and I wonder if my compressions are at fault.

I hear the sirens now, two of them, and soon the flashing lights are near. I'm still cracking ribs on a corpse, pumping maniacally like an idiot, dropping down every thirty compressions to puff air into his bloody mouth. I collapse as soon as the first two paramedics arrive. The next crew attends to me, the woman stopping for a moment when she looks at my face. She breaks out a large gauze pad to hold over my nose hole.

—Darren? Get over here. Help me look.

They begin to part the long grass around me, and it takes me a minute to realize they're looking for my long-lost nose, the little nub of flesh long since passed through the tract of a pit bull. I pull the bloody pad away to show them.

—This is his blood. I'm fine.

At intake, my interviewer feebly danced around questions both obvious and forbidden. I had my bachelor's, criminology courses out of the Justice Institute, and three years doing volunteer security work at the Jazz Fest. I buried everyone else on the POPAT with the fastest run in my group. He praised my achievements, but I could tell there was more he wanted to ask.

—Do you think you would be comfortable here?

I took my time answering, rooting through my pockets for a Kleenex to wipe my leaky nose hole.

—Do you think I'd be comfortable anywhere?

The class photo was fantastic, all the pretty boys and girls, then me, the monster at the end of the row, showing more teeth than usual.

I sit in the mud with a bloody gauze pad in my hand, two paramedics standing on either side of me. Flashing lights imply urgency, but with the biker gone, there's no reason to move quickly, no reason to move at all.

—So, hit-and-run?

I look up at her, angry that she's tipped the balance of silence with her question. Darren drapes a red fleece blanket around me while they both wait for my words, truth from an officer of the law. Clearly there was some hitting and some running. Darren has a bright-orange fauxhawk and I wonder how many times he's been asked by supervisors to switch to a more conventional look. Would it be implied, hinted at, to avoid a harassment issue? How many unconscious people would come to, see his head, and wonder if they were hallucinating? I have no obligation to answer their questions, no reason to feel uncomfortable. It doesn't really matter what happened here, because I'll be the one asking the questions.

—I'll be the one asking the questions.

—Okay, chief, can we help you up at least?

—I'm good.

She looks at her partner, shrugs, and starts to pack up her gear. When they're gone, I call for the CSU, and turn up the heat in the car. Another cruiser with flashers on comes roaring over the crest of the hill. Arnot slows, then pulls alongside, our cars almost touching.

—Angelo called my cell. He wanted me to come around and make sure you were okay. You're okay, right? He said you guys stumbled onto a pretty nasty hit-and-run. It was a hit-and-run, right? You gonna say anything, Face?

I stare at him for a few seconds, then roll up the window. Arnot yells at the glass while I shield my face with my hand.

—Clement has a family, you know!

Arnot turns his car around and speeds off. In all this time there hasn't been a single civilian car in or out of the park, as if the universe is shutting out any distractions or contaminants at the scene. The crow is screeching again. I don't know what he's saying, but I'm pretty sure that later in the day he'll share it with one or two thousand of his friends as they start their daily migration west over Burnaby. Perhaps it will be a simple story about a man putting a yellow marker next to a bottle in the bush.

THE SCHADENFREUDE RAIL

YOU DON'T NEED 350 HORSE TO TOW A SKI boat, but Reynold still enjoys the show of excess, the big Dodge Ram roaring up the ramp, the matching boat and trailer sucked from the water in seconds. Farah turns away from his explanation of Hemi technology, tracking a passing gull. They both look back to the truck when the door opens and the young sunburnt owner swings down from the cab and swaggers down the slope to inspect the dripping rig, barely glancing at the gawkers on the Schadenfreude Rail. At 40K for the truck and more for the boat, Reynold wonders where a guy like that finds the money. Sure, you can make forty bucks an hour swinging a hammer but this kid looks like he's barely out of high school. More likely he's a smug little gangster growing weed in a mould-filled basement, or running a few phone-sex lines, drawing out middle-aged ejaculate in dark rooms across the city. If the shiny ski boat is Dad's, it's an odd choice for an old man. The truck has those ram stencils over the taillights, and it looks like the winch wire's never been off the drum. Swagger's the type who will brag about max payload but won't help a friend move because it might scratch the box. Farah used to giggle as Reynold gutted sheeple, but once again he is staring at the back of her head. She shrugs off his hand when he lays it lightly on her shoulder.

Reynold and Farah watch with twenty others as More Money Than Brains attempts to back up his trailer. He overshoots to each side, taking it too fast, skidding to a stop, then pulling forward to straighten the trailer before his next botched attempt. He weaves like a drunk down to the waterline, his wife calling out directions and flashing a baffling collection of hand signals that he ignores, until the trailer rests at forty-five degrees to the water's edge. The rail crowd responds with murmured criticism and shaking heads. Farah once enjoyed Reynold's low, running commentary on the undeserving rich, the toys they can barely operate, their failure to live magazine dreams. The boaters may see envy when they look up, but the rail crowd is here to watch things go wrong, just like NASCAR.

Tattoo entertains his girlfriends in a sleek white Four Winns cruiser. He wears a catalogue of body-ink clichés: barbed wire, tribal signs, dragons, and an eagle with a hint of Third Reich. A Harley blasts out the mouth of a flaming skull. It's not actually written on his body, but it's clear he would like people to believe he's a fierce young rebel who lives to ride and rides to live. The engine is off, and they don't seem hurried or impatient. Reynold had assumed they were waiting for another, but maybe the plan is to spend their time tied to the dock, looking good and being envied from a distance by gawking fools. Tiny triangles of fabric cover the female parts that must be covered, but everything else is on display.

Delusions about the local climate can be indulged at the dock, but out on the water, at speed, they'll be cold. California is still a thousand klicks to the south.

It isn't hard to spot the straggler crossing the parking lot, lookin' so gangsta, straight from the rough, gritty streets of Burnaby. Cap turned backwards, heavy gold chain, baggy pants, crisp Timberlands—buddy missed it by a decade, yo. He packs beer onto the boat, inexplicably proud of his beverages, how many will be consumed, how quickly, the likely results. They cast off their lines and idle out into the bay, oblivious to the posts that mark the edge of the channel. Tattoo wants to go where there are no other boats, taking a sharp turn to starboard without considering why there are no other boats. With the bow stuck in the mud, he gives it full throttle, as though that will somehow save them, push them through this. The prop dredges mud, and the rail crowd ponders his thought process, what little there may be. It's a few minutes of angry confusion before Tattoo realizes he can simply put it in reverse and back out the way he came. He wanted to go east very badly, right over the mud flats, but the mud didn't care where he wanted to go. In the interest of keeping the body count down, someone should idle alongside and pull the keys from his dash. He's just too dumb to run a boat. Couples chatter, point, and smirk, cheered that new heights in stupid have been reached so early in the day, with hours of fun to go.

Farah pulls back slightly and studies the people on the rail now, not just the boaters. Someone took a wrong turn and got stuck in the mud, an easy mistake, especially for someone not familiar with the area. Everything east of the markers goes dry in low tide, but if you were inexperienced you might not know this. Full throttle was the wrong reaction, but there was no damage to the boat or the passengers, and the situation was quickly resolved. You'd never guess that from the reaction on the rail. A drop of blood falls in the water and sharks circle. Reynold makes her face sag. Close to him she feels extreme gravity, a black hole that breaks her down. The light spirit that is sucked into his vortex has no effect on his mood. Positive energy is simply destroyed. She cringes as he stakes out the next target in his teardown universe.

Farah spends too much time thinking about men who aren't Reynold, specifically Amalio, her olive-skinned, curly-haired coworker, who lacks any of the resentment one might find appropriate or understandable coming from an under-moneyed, overeducated, thirty-nine-year-old barista. Every day he faces Jabba, a giant, ranting complaint dispenser, with no other thought than the alleviation of her suffering. Even as she drones on about coffee that is too hot or not hot enough, and flecks of spittle alight on the counter, someone else's beverage, and Amalio from head to waist, there is nothing that looks like anger or impatience on his face. Only he can see inside, past her folds of fat, to the hurt that makes her what she is, and calm her with a look that says, This isn't really about coffee, is it? It's about you. The compassionate Buddha smiles even as his eyes, nose and mouth are potentially infected with whatever might travel on Jabba's spit.

When Amalio cleans the espresso machine, nothing else exists. Every two hours he scrubs old oils out of the porta-filter, cleans the steam wand, and wipes down the entire unit with the gentle grace of a Japanese tea ceremony. The wonky bottom drawer that she must jerk, twist, and pummel, easily complies with his touch, his hands that feel what the drawer needs in order to open.

Farah prays for every customer to leave. In the afternoons, and sometimes midmorning, the place clears out, and Amalio's focus turns to her in a surge of energy that runs up and down her spine, making her feel lighter and taller. The first time he touched her she was bent over, wrestling with the filter drawer, and he tapped the small of her back to let her know he was passing behind her. Sometimes at the punch line of a joke, he'll touch her forearm. Last week he didn't predict that Reynold would forget her birthday, but he was ready with a paper crown and a cupcake with an inch of pink icing. He stood behind her, adjusting the size of the crown, close enough to kiss the back of her neck. Then he spent three minutes fussing over her latte, brushing her portrait into the surface.

The accident told Farah exactly nothing. Three months ago, bright lights lit up the right side of her car as she passed through the intersection of Austin and Schoolhouse, just before a drunk driver T-boned her. Post-accident, post-airbag, she expected a brief window of clarity regarding the direction of her life. A sudden death avoided was supposed to transform your thinking, so she waited patiently for her revelation while the traffic light cycled through its colours and the drunk made a slow-speed getaway with his caved front end and wobbly wheel.

She started to feel the abrasions on her face from the airbag about the same time she realized she was alone and no traffic was coming from either direction. Her teeth hurt as if they had been slammed together. She had learned how jarring it could be when expected direction did not match actual direction, but nothing was revealed other than the indifference of her fellow man. She was waiting for a message, but she already knew what she wanted it to be: leave Reynold. She needed a good reason, and a ground-shaking shift in all her assumptions should have resulted from the crash, but leaving Reynold was no revelation. It was an item on a to-do list, another chore she had avoided for over a year.

Reynold must go because Amalio never tells her not to use her hands so much when she's telling a story. Because Amalio doesn't caution her against telling strangers too much personal information. Because Amalio does not insist on approving her wardrobe before she leaves the house for a drink with friends, or criticize the way she stacks dirty dishes, or belittle her job. Once, there was a list of things she liked about Reynold, but now, watching him in profile as he sneers at another hapless boater, she can't remember one.

Reynold resents how Farah's fluctuating blood-sugar levels transform her from fluffy kitten to claws-out street cat. She begins to tow him toward Larry's Fish and Chips because food intake must happen now, but apparently there's still time to bend down and pet a mini-Labradoodle. The owner has dreads halfway down his back and wears mismatched athletic clothes and a pair of stinking Jesus sandals. Dogs suck. They're stupid, loud, and smelly. People buy them to get the protection, loyalty, and obedience they can't get from other people. Reynold wonders what kind of man has a dog the size of a rat. If a man has to have a dog, it better be higher than knee level. Farah seems to be flirting with this loser, sweet with him when she'd be blood-sugar grumpy if it were just Reynold.

Farah would love a dog like this, but of course that wouldn't be allowed by He Who Controls Everything. And the dog loves Farah, licking salt off her hands, wagging his tail, putting his paws up on her knees. Dogs just love, that's what they do, and if you ran into a bear on the trail your dog would go after it, defend you to the death. Nothing brings strangers together faster than a friendly, happy dog. The hippy is not her type, but it's interesting how anyone picked at random from the crowd is usually a lot nicer than her boyfriend.

Reynold sees Dreads glance down at Farah's chest, the two of them acting as if he isn't even there, as if he doesn't exist. He grabs her arm and drags her away, Dreads concerned but rooted. She shakes off his grip and checks for bruises as they silently walk to Larry's. He wishes she'd stop being so dramatic.

Larry's is packed. Why don't they hire more cooks? Was he surprised by a crowd showing up at the park on a hot, sunny Saturday? With twenty numbers to go before Reynold's comes up, it's obvious Larry has enough business to hire another person or two, unless he's too greedy, anxious to squeeze every dime out of the place. Farah won't stop examining her bruise, oblivious to everything else. She seems reluctant to pay, pulling out her purse only when Reynold stuffs his hands in his pockets and stares at her.

Being cheap seems odd for someone who's getting a big fat insurance cheque. No doubt she thinks she earned that money. Reynold takes a sip of his drink and sets it back down on the counter.

—This is Pepsi. I ordered Coke.

—Coke, Pepsi, same difference, right?

—Pepsi is not Coke.

Farah should have seen this coming, because it happens often enough. A dozen hungry people in line behind them will no doubt appreciate this age-old conflict between the duelling colas. Reynold lectures, building his rage as Larry appears at the takeout window. Farah takes a half step away from them, then another, each step feeling better than the last. Away from the window she is able to detach from this as Reynold raises his arms and Larry starts jabbing the air with his finger. Reynold eventually rejoins Farah at the rail without any food from Larry's. He's taken a principled stand, and she's ready to collapse from hunger.

—Thanks for your support back there.

—Black holes don't need support.

—What?

—Nothing.

Amalio ascended to god-like status for three reasons. First, he noticed right away, from Farah's posture at the counter, that the accident had knocked her out of alignment, twisted and torqued her joints and muscles, disrupting her equilibrium. Second, he was willing to do something about it. Third, what he did was extremely effective. Minutes after Farah complained about her stiff neck, he pressed his thumb hard into the muscle knot, making her cry out.

No customers were there to hear, so he dug in a second time and she nearly fell to her knees. The relief that followed the initial pain proved he was hitting the spot. He thought it might be better if he could get her up against the wall to give her more support, so she leaned against the doorframe of the washroom as he took another run at it. He didn't have to look or fumble around. He knew exactly where the tension was and he laid into it. Every few hours, for the next few days, they waited for the café to empty.

A brain-dead woman is waiting for her husband to position their launched boat next to where she stands on the dock. The engine won't start because the mixture's too rich, and he's drifting down on an unoccupied boat. Brain Dead doesn't seem to realize how things are coming together. All she needs to do is step onto the empty boat and fend off their boat so the hulls won't get scratched. He can't do it because he's at the controls, trying to get the engine started. Brain Dead could save the day, fending off the boat and guiding it to an empty spot, but she just stands there, as useful as a post—less useful . . . at least you can tie something to a post. Sure, not everyone has nautical skills, but this one fails at the lowest level of common sense.

Now Speedy's coming in too fast, trying to impress the crowd with his approach, but the breeze pushes him off course and he hits the rollers of his trailer at a bad angle. The boat flies up the trailer right to the winch, but it's off-centre with a ten-degree list. The boat is hooked on the trailer at the stern, so he can't power it off using the engine, and his helpers seem unable to push it off. All three of them stare at it as if their combined concentration could form some kind of mental tractor beam that would move their boat into position. Meanwhile, on the crest of the slope, others wait to launch. It gets better. The driver of the truck backs up to re-float the boat, dropping the trailer off the cement ridge at the end of the ramp. He moves forward again, and the ridge acts like a set of tire chocks. He guns it and the wheels start spinning, more gas, more spinning. It says 4WD on the side of the truck, but he must not have thought to engage it. He can't back up and take a run at it, because that will launch the boat into the air when it pops up over the ridge and possibly damage the trailer. Another lengthy stand-and-stare session for Speedy and the gang.

Farah has hope for the North River workboat that's heading for the ramp. Crab traps and mounted fishing-rod holders suggest competence. The wife backed the trailer down earlier with minimum fuss, slow but straight down to the water. He comes in at a steady speed, crabs his approach angle to adjust for the wind, straightens at the last second, and slides smoothly up the rollers, stopping about a foot from the winch. The wife's ready with the hook, snapping it in before the boat can backslide and winching it to the rubber stopper. A converted cynic on the rail claps. Reynold is silenced while he searches for the error, hoping the guy will forget to tilt the motor forward before dragging the boat out of the water. It's a ten-out-of-ten operation and Reynold has nothing to say.

—Whatever.

No, not whatever, Farah thinks. You've got to be able to take the good with the bad. Sometimes people know what they're doing. Sometimes you've got to give credit. This event, this shining, perfect event deserves more than whatever. They worked as a team, bringing that boat in as they had probably done dozens of times before. Chances are they enjoyed themselves out there, the wife peering over the bow at her reflection in the flat, calm water, the husband enjoying the high tones of his perfectly maintained and operated engine as they motored up Indian Arm for a quiet picnic lunch of goat cheese, fruit, and Raincoast Crisps. That's what fun is, not standing on the sidelines and criticizing everything.

Amalio would be good in a boat. He'd tinker and caress their sputtering old outboard until it ran again and that victory, bringing the damn thing back from the dead, would be more fun than if it had never broken down. He'd be fully there, loving everything, coiling a line with the same pleasure with which he'd rub lotion on her back. They'd be fine with no words, rocking gently in their little rented skiff.

The deep, sickening crack is the sound of a boat that has broken its spine. Every head on the rail swings toward the large, inboard overnighter that just slid off the back of a trailer onto the cement. Reynold thrills to the technical challenges facing the driver, who comes out screaming, unwilling to own this one. The object of blame is the teenager near the winch. The driver can't back it into the water because the weight of the boat is resting on the skeg. He can't winch the boat back onto the trailer because it's too heavy. His only option is to stare at this magnificent display of incompetence until someone with skills and intelligence shows up.

Farah watches Reynold reach deep-hearted ecstasy. The teenager is paralyzed, shocked by the scope of the damage. The father is not taking in any input from anyone or anything. His world has changed; his day is ruined; a hot red flush of embarrassment spreads across his face. A more experienced man, maybe someone waiting to launch, should come down and talk to the guy, put a hand on his shoulder and tell him, this is what we're going to do. Some kind man with strong hands and a big truck with a winch in front could come down here and pull that boat back into the cradle. We stop to help the lady who tripped and landed on her groceries, or the kid who didn't quite pull off the stunt on his skateboard. We rush over and we ask if they're all right, but no one on the rail is going to do that, not today.

Reynold watches Farah walk away on those ridiculous lime-green wedge shoes she insists on wearing. She has strange ideas about what's attractive, and if men sometimes turn and stare is it because they like what they see or they can't believe someone that young could have such hideous taste? If your income allows you to dress better than your white-trash peers, why not donate that slutty miniskirt and buy something an adult would wear? And hoop earrings? Seriously? This one's broken, untrainable, more trouble than she's worth. Sure, maybe she has a big insurance cheque coming, but he's already bored with the sex, and she already wants to change him. It's a doomed effort, but for tonight at least, they'll share the same bed. Between now and then they're in for exhausting repairs, patching it together one more time.

The seat belt had held Farah tight long past the impact. She opened her door and twisted the key to turn off the chime. She didn't know it, but it would be the last time she would see her faithful six-year-old Cavalier. For the first time she thought the name odd. Why not a Buick Indignant or a Ford Sarcastic? Over the ticking sound of the cooling metal, she could hear the drunk that hit her making his walking-speed getaway in a small, crappy car that was making a horrible, most definitely terminal, grinding sound. After that it was quiet. A cool, fresh wind blew down the street, scrubbed clean by fir trees in Mundy Park, perhaps. She took in the smell of cut grass and the very faint sound of someone's wind chimes. A light turned on over the steps of a nearby house, and it wasn't long before a man about her father's age was there to help her, to ask quietly if she was all right, if she was bleeding. He didn't watch from the window, point and laugh until the ambulance came. He didn't leave her lying in a cradle of broken glass and twisted metal. After he checked to see that she wasn't bleeding out, he held her hand lightly and asked her again if she was okay. Together they listened to the sirens get louder, because that's what people do.

NEW

THE LAST TIME MERCER CHECKED A trash bag in the middle of his field it was full of dead kittens. He automatically thought of Nathan Wills, the neighbour's kid, doing donuts on his field, wrecking crops, until the black garbage bag came sliding out over the dropped tailgate, the kid too drunk to notice or care. What other explanation was there? If you didn't want to burn your trash, or take it to the dump, you chucked it in the ditch, or in the woods. No one sane and sober would take the time to dump a single trash bag in the middle of his field. It may have been unfair to blame the kid every time a shovel went missing or someone backed into a fence post, but it was easy, so things mysterious attached themselves to Nathan, a sixteen-year-old alcoholic.

Mercer walks over the stubble toward another black garbage bag. He squints, his eyes reluctant to accept that the semi-transparent, shredded crepe material forms a sack shape but is not a plastic bag. He slows, more confused, his foot sinking into something squishy. His boot tread is filled with mashed guts that trail off into a tail. He uses a pen to pick it out and then notices three more creatures, moving slowly through the stubble. On his knees he moves closer to the nearest one, which looks like a small halibut with the tail of a stingray. The speckled bumps resemble fish scales, but closer in he sees it's the rough texture of the skin. Two slits near the tail open, and red powder puffs out in superfine particles, practically aerosol. It makes him sneeze. He turns the thing over with a stick, revealing dozens of short white stalks that move in coordinated waves. The word peristalsis comes to mind, however inaccurate. Creepy and beautiful.

The creatures seem to move together, and drawing a line from the black sack to their current location, it looks like they're headed for the ditch. Beyond the road there is another stubbled hay field, bush, then the river. Kat takes her time getting to the site, unaffected by Mercer's excited tone on the phone. She brings a shovel. He didn't ask her to bring a shovel. Her truck is still running, the door open, the annoying chime telling them so, while Kat stands over the things, stern-faced and ready.

—What are they?

—I don't know. I think they're new. What's the shovel for?

—I'm going to smash them.

—Why?

—They might breed. They might eat crops. They might be dangerous.

Mercer grabs the shovel from her and stands between her and the things.

—You don't know that. They could be perfectly harmless.

—Okay, but you remember this moment and what you did

when there were only three of them.

Kat yells over her shoulder as she walks back to the truck: Ernie is coming on Wednesday at nine to look at the PTO on the tractor, and Wendy called from the bank. By this time, Walter has seen two trucks stopped by the road, one with the door open, and two people standing in the middle of the field staring down at something. He simply can't pass by. He meets Kat halfway.

—Everything okay, Kat?

—Everything's fine, Walter. Mercer made some friends. They're new.

—What do you mean, new?

—Go check it out for yourself.

Walter is the first to be ready to help out a neighbour, whatever is required. Walter will also be the first to update everyone he meets on the status of an event in the middle of Mercer's field.

—Looks like a grouper.

—It doesn't look anything like a grouper. It looks like a halibut fish with a stingray's tail.

—Nope, looks like a marbled grouper.

The two men eventually agree that what the things look like has nothing to do with what they are. Walter claims they must be amphibians, given their fish-like body shape, possibly nocturnal, most certainly used to much warmer climates. The barb on the tail is probably poisonous. He makes many more conclusions and assumptions about the creatures because neither Mercer nor the creatures can dispute any of it. Mercer asks Walter to keep this to himself, which he does on the quiet walk back to his truck, but only because his cell phone is in the glove compartment and there's no one in yelling distance.

Turns out Mercer's concerns about secrecy are overblown. No flood of nosey neighbours appears within the hour or the next three. There's something new in the middle of his field on this bright October morning, and no one seems to care. Later, Kat calls to say that his dinner has been prepared, served, then wrapped and refrigerated. Around sunset he goes back to the house for a flashlight, a blanket, and a lawn chair. At three in the morning he wishes he'd brought his jacket as well. He heads back to the house and tries to slip into bed without waking Kat. He spends an hour staring at the ceiling, thinking about the creatures, then heads back out to the site. Kat calls at six to tell him that breakfast has been prepared and then thrown in the garbage. Also, the gate isn't going to fix itself, Wendy called again about the line of credit, and Ernie is coming tomorrow to look at the PTO on the tractor. Mercer has to be there to show him what's wrong with it, and the guy gets three hundred dollars just for showing up, whether he works on the thing or not, you know? Also, it's time to clean the shop. She spent half an hour looking for the oil filter wrench and had to use a bicycle chain instead.

Nathan Wills is suddenly there, and Mercer, startled, kicks over his thermos.

—What you got there?

Mercer stands to get between the kid and the creatures. What you got there? Coming out of any other mouth it wouldn't cause concern, but when the kid smiles you know somehow, somewhere, someone has been or will be hurt, robbed, or lied to. He stands with his hands behind his back, idle and twitchy. There's nothing but a trail of damage behind the kid, some of it minor but all of it bad, like a long black smear that tars the landscape. The kid's hands are coming out. His hands are coming out from around his back and Mercer will have to react in some way, to protect the creatures or himself. The hands come out with a phone and Mercer wonders where he stole it.

Mercer can't allow the creatures to be covered by a trail of tar, but he's so desperate to show them off that he takes the kid's interest at face value. It's possible the kid is interested in something other than himself this one time. Mercer can't restrain his fatherly pride, showing the speckled skin that changes colour, the mesmerizing motion tentacles on the underside, the tiny red powder clouds that puff out when you get too close. He looks up midsentence and the kid is gone.

Mercer calculates that the current course and speed will put the little guys at the edge of the road at around five o'clock, half an hour from now. If they feel vibrations when heavy trucks pass, they might have the brains to know what that means, to recognize that as a hazard, but he's unwilling to gamble their lives on that. Left alone, they would struggle with the gravel for a while until the vibration was detected, the sun would disappear for a quarter second, and then they'd be one with the tire tread. He feels like an ambassador, guiding the little guys away from danger, keeping them safe in their new environment. He races back to the house for a bucket and a spatula when they're fifteen minutes from crossing. Sure, it's undignified, and a very baffled Jennifer Muir will have a story after she passes slowly by, trying to make sense of the things in Mercer's hand, but the only thing to do is to flip them into the bucket and transfer them to the other side of the road.

Mercer shivers in the dark, praying for someone, a wife even, to bring him a ham sandwich and strong coffee. Catnaps in the chair do little to relieve the fatigue that pulls him down like extra gravity. He was expecting a little support. He assumed there would be just a little understanding, even though his mission can't be explained and perhaps isn't rational or productive. Does a smooth marriage depend on restricting himself to a very narrow range of activities? The little guys push on, although the cold seems to slow them down. Maybe a ten-degree drop would be fatal. Mercer isn't taking a chance tonight, especially with the frost warning. First, he tries a layer of hay, but when he peeks under, they've almost stopped. Next he goes back to the house and picks up the global warmer. Heating the outdoors is stupid, but Kat likes the patio heater because it "takes the edge off" after sunset. Why not put on a sweater, like people have been doing for centuries? No, she's got to fire up a propane torch and heat everything within a twenty-foot radius. She's sure to be first in line for the outdoor air-conditioning units as soon as the wizards in the create-demand-out-of-nothing department realize the potential market. Tonight the global warmer saves lives, the glowing red beacon reviving the little guys, who start moving forward again, all except one.

Kat calls mid-morning to scold Mercer for missing Ernie's call. Ernie checked the PTO and there appeared to be nothing wrong with it. She tried to imitate the noise it made under load but that just made him laugh. He left, insisting it was fine.

—Fuck all that! Fuck the PTO, and the bank, and the gate, and the shop, and whatever else you got lined up. I just want to do this one thing. Can I have this one thing?

—There are a lot of things I want that I can't have. I'm trying to run a farm here. Single-handed, apparently. There's stuff that's got to be done, and you're not helping.

—What has it been, a couple of days? Is everything so fragile it will fall apart if I'm gone for a couple of days? There's something special happening out here, Kat. Can you look up from your daily grind long enough to be curious?

Twenty years, over seven thousand days running this farm and a few days off is too much. How is that different from slavery? What if he needed a week off? Or a month? What if he wanted to spend half a year in Australia? Someone calls Mercer and he turns around. Simon, with the look of a wholesome farm kid, claims to be a scientist from the University of Regina. The clip on YouTube was forwarded to him by a colleague whose son had been showing all his friends. The tag listed Bethune as the location, and once in town, Simon was directed by a gas-station attendant and one of Mercer's neighbours. Simon stops talking when he sees them.

—Oh, my god!

A man with a degree, an educated man, who came all the way from Regina to Mercer's field, gets down on his hands and knees and puts his face inches away from the creatures.

—Oh, my god!

Mercer doesn't know science, but that doesn't sound like a very scientific thing to say.

—It looks a bit like a giant Triops, but it isn't.

Red powder puffs into his face and he stumbles back, wiping it off.

—Don't worry, it's harmless. It might make you sneeze but that's all.

Mercer takes Simon out in the field to see the sack. When Mercer glances back to the road he sees Kat's truck stopped close to the global warmer. As soon as she lifts the shovel from the back of the truck they're off, Mercer with a head start, Simon trailing him, shouting questions that are ignored. Kat's a little faster, carrying the shovel at shoulder height like a spear. She slows in the area where the creatures are and starts searching. Mercer is close, but not fast enough to stop her from raising her shovel high and slamming it down. She raises it again, but Mercer grabs it and twists her around his hips until she lets go and falls over. She's strong, something he had forgotten. He stands over her with the shovel in his hands. He almost never sees her in anything other than jeans and a T-shirt. In the fall she adds a jean jacket. In the winter she switches to a Carhartt with a thick lining. One time, the hottest day this summer, she wore an undershirt while digging in the garden, unaware of the well-defined muscles in her back and shoulders and the effect they had on him. Everything is fragile and fleeting. How did he ever think otherwise? You can't protect any one thing from the forces arrayed against it. You can only enjoy it while it's here. She lies in the dirt, stunned by his force. She scrambles away, without turning her back on him, and walks the rest of the way to the truck. He follows her, reaches into the cab, and holds the gearshift in park.

—That guy back there is a scientist. He came to look at the creature that you just mashed into the ground. What the hell is wrong with you? That's a scientist from the university and he came all the way out here to look at those things, and all you can think to do is mash one into the ground like it's a clump of goddamn manure.

—You stay out here and play with your freaky friends all you want, Mercer. It doesn't really matter, because Wendy won't extend our line of credit. You figure out how to stitch together another year. I'm going to my sister's for a while. Have fun with the farm.

Kat takes advantage of Mercer's shock, pulling the stick down into drive and roaring off, the tires shooting stones and dirt at him and into the grill of his truck. Of course a life can fall apart, but it's the speed of it that's dizzying. Kat and Wendy are the same: for years you make contributions, and then you have a little rough spot and suddenly you're shit in their eyes. Everything you built, everything you did is nothing.

—Mercer, is that your dog?

Simon is pointing to Mercer's German shepherd, Thunder, who holds one of the creatures in his mouth. Oh, it's a fun game for Thunder, yes it is, yes it is. The red powder makes Thunder sneeze, but he's not letting go of his new toy, no he isn't. Mercer steps forward and Thunder takes a crouched stance, ready to run. Mercer freezes and Simon calls out from his position, too scared to move.

—He's going to bury that somewhere, isn't he?

When the two men move at the same time, Thunder is gone. There are no remaining creatures, not even the one Kat splattered, probably snatched by Thunder while Mercer was fighting with her. The only thing left to show Simon is the crepe sack. The black tissue crumbles easily between Simon's fingers, and he mumbles to himself as if Mercer isn't there, taking measurements, photos and samples. He asks the question, to no one in particular:

—If this is the birthing sac, how big is the mother?

Simon looks at Mercer for the answer, then over his shoulder, nervously. Crickets are the biggest threat, and they don't seem to be organized. The occasional bee flies past in wide, lazy turns, committed only to pollinating. Tires sing on the highway, distant, gentle, soothing. There are no clear threats to Mercer's territory, and nothing left for him to do in the middle of the stubbled hay field. He is free, for now, to carry on.

BEHAVIOUR BEFITTING A YOUNG MAN

ANY CAR BURNS PLENTY OF GAS GOING over the Coquihalla, but Gibson's Datsun has been especially gluttonous. At first he thought it was the weight of his stuff resting heavily on the back springs. In the less-crowded corner of a scenic lookout, with the painfully bright mountains at his back, he stares at an engine that withholds its secrets. Fifty klicks later, on his hands and knees, he finds a wide, wet strip along the bottom of the gas tank. A semi rolls by, the gust flapping his shirt and blowing dust into his eyes. The money he's budgeted for food and lodging will now be spent on gas.

He wonders what the B stands for in Datsun B210. B-grade? Beware? Botched? If the gas leak were the only problem, he might be able to forgive the old girl, but he suspects it's short a cylinder going uphill, full power kicking in only as he levels off at the top, when it's no longer needed. Another surprise: driving over water at high speed creates fender fountains, high arcs of spray that blast through rusted-out crevices on either side of the hood. The floor feels spongy because large sections of it are gone. If you pull up the carpet you can see a scary amount of road.

Gas stations are farther and farther apart. Math formulas with too many variables cycle through his head: the range of the car, the range of the car with a hole or holes in the tank, the added load going uphill, balanced by greater economy on the way down.

EVEN AFTER TWO WEEKS OF restless change, he had to admit it was a child's room. The mini-basketball hoop from the back of the door was down, along with the volleyball trophies. Even the aquarium had been banished to the garage. Still, the bed was a twin, a good size for someone who never had overnight guests. The books that remained on the shelves were bright and colourful ... juvenile. The computer would stay, its drive full of games that no longer interested him. The car was full anyway.

He stood for a moment at the door to his parents' room. He and his sister hung there on the wall over the bureau, looking awkward and out of place, framed by the flowers at Butchart Gardens. In the corner, a set of golf clubs his father could not bear to store in the garage. His mother's jumble of shoes, kicked into the closet from across the room with enough force to leave black marks on the closet wall.

His sister's room was across from his. It might be days before she knew he was gone. Her room was merely a place to put all the stuffed animals given to her by boys who came and went so often that no one bothered to remember their names. There was enough of her to say goodbye to in that room, in the tangles of clothing, the empty hamster cage. The electric guitar, still prized but rarely touched, was how she would become the next Bif Naked.

Gibson's car sat idling as he rang Chelsea's doorbell. She went crazy, listing the many reasons why his plan was wrong, stupid, selfish. After half an hour of this she was too exhausted to resist a lingering hug, observed, of course, by her mother, who spied on them from a crack between the curtains. Chelsea shook her head at the sight of his raggedy clothes pressed flat against the window and quickly walked back to the house so he would not see her cry.

Toby was at basketball practice. There were others he could call on a Saturday morning: Tony, Brian, Samantha. There were better, kinder ways to make a new start but instead, he pulled away from the curb and drove to the end of the street, where he spent a few minutes staring at the stop sign before turning onto the highway.

THE CAR WHEEZES TO THE top of another mountain pass and lines up for a straight stretch down a steep grade. Near the bottom, sun glints off the windscreen of a car parked by the side of the road. Gibson squints to make out a cop looking down into the scope of his radar.

Even with both hands, he can't make second. The teeth grind together, kicking out the stick—he's already going too fast. It takes two good stomps and to-the-floor pressure to get the slightest braking action. The emergency brake has always been burnt out. There's nothing left to try. He can't rest against the bumper of a semi. The runaway lane would probably rip the wheels off. Swerving back and forth would scrub off some speed—and make him look drunk.

At twenty klicks over the limit he gives it the double pump. Gibson expects the cop to point him to the shoulder but he turns away from the radar and goes back to his car. Gibson flies by and the cop turns around, judging the car's speed with an expert eye, but he's too far away from the tripod to clock it. Gibson climbs higher, in the slowest getaway ever, hoping to do the first third of the hill on momentum alone. He needs to delay the moment when he has to rev it up, puffing out a huge plume of oily blue smoke, gassing everyone behind him. If the cop sees that, the mission is over; the old bomber will be declared unfit for the road, a health hazard, a death trap.

On Friday, Mr. Hind wanted to know where Gibson had put the rubber mallets. Every few months Gibson moved them from between the caulk guns and the paint to their logical place beside the hammers. He would do it when Hind was out, hoping he wouldn't notice. The carpentry area naturally divided into things that hit, things that cut, and things you used to slap on paint or goop. Hind recognized no such logic. All he would say was that the paint aisle was the place for mallets. That's where they went. That's where they'd been since opening day.

Hind reminded him that if he wanted to be manager some-day, he'd have to start using his head. A little common sense, you know? Hind would expect stupid mistakes from Jerry, but Gibson was being groomed, and someday, if everything went well, if he continued to work hard, if he studied the day-to-day operations, if he did all that, someday he'd manage the place.

The first time Gibson heard about the manager position, he almost snorted. The job was beneath him. Otherwise, why the hell was he going to school? But it wasn't long before the horror of aiming for the middle was replaced by a series of what-ifs. He began running calculations based on his guess at a manager's wages. So-and-so many hours equalled an apartment with so-and-so many square feet. Car payments at so many dollars per month, so many years in debt. And way off in the distance, too far to think about, a house.

Yes, Hind made it clear that the job was waiting for Gibson, assuming he would someday be able to do things Hind's way, the right way. Rubber mallets did not belong next to the hammers. The scolding, Gibson was to understand, was something to be grateful for, the kind of correction poor Jerry would never receive.

Gibson put on his apron, and nodded at everything Mr. Hind said. There were mallets that needed to be moved and a guy poking around the garden hoses who looked like he needed some help. Hind cocked his chin over to the guy, as Gibson clearly needed some direction.

He didn't hate Hind or the job, but that day he became painfully aware that while he was inside counting nails or explaining how to use a plane, there were people outside engaging with the real world. The thought of staying in Kamloops without even sampling a small part of the rest of the country seemed unspeakably depressing. Hind's nostrils flared with irritation. Gibson said he couldn't work there anymore. Noooooo, Hind said, his mouth holding the shape as he fell silent. Noooooo. That's exactly how he said it as he held a sprinkler loosely, its place on the shelf forgotten. Gibson moved toward the door. Behind him Hind said he could leave the mallets where they were. Wherever he wanted to put them was fine. Hind said some other things, but by that time the door had closed and Gibson was noticing perfect summer clouds, breathing fresh air, like a free person with an open future.

LINES OF PAINT, REFLECTIVE STRIPS, markers and signs suggest a course of travel on the highway, but ultimately it's Gibson who decides. Nothing can stop him from going straight where a turn is indicated. Little force is required to change his course completely. He'll take this road as suggested. That's his choice today. Views that deserve half an hour get half a second, because the beast is running well, and killing momentum now is too risky. His neck hurts from craning his head around to catch scenes that fly by as the car ducks into tunnels and out again, into the bursting white.

THE CAR HAD BEEN SITTING in the guy's driveway for more than a year. The For Sale sign—one of those plastic ones you buy at Canadian Tire off a spinning rack—looked faded and brittle. It was one of the many markers Gibson would glance at on his way to work. The old beast still had air in all the tires, glass in all the windows, and it was pointed downhill on the driveway, as if eager to go. Later Gibson learned the owner parked it that way for an easy jump start.

On Friday morning Gibson stopped at the foot of the driveway. There was no time for a break, as he always timed his commute down to the second. The longer he stood, the faster he'd have to run to make it to work on time. The body was badly rusted from winter salt, and the paint had faded to a matte finish. It wasn't pretty, but he could tell it wanted to be used.

He walked up the steps and knocked on the door. He planned to wait half a minute, then walk away, giving himself points for spontaneity. The seal on the door popped abruptly and the scruffy-faced, overweight owner appeared.

—Yeah?

—How much for the car?

In Chilliwack, Gibson is getting gas for what seems like the ten thousandth time. Two weeks of funds have already gone out the pipe in a messy blue cloud. A rivulet of gas trickles under his shoe before making its way to the gutter. He's used two paper-towel rolls trying to staunch the leak, stuffing the sheets wherever they'll fit, and still it keeps coming.

—Hey, is that gas coming out of your car?

Gibson answers without looking down.

—No, that's a puddle of water.

—No, man, that's gas. You've got a major gas leak. I've got to report this. You have to stay here while I report this.

After the gas jockey strides toward the office, Gibson sticks a twenty between the nozzle and its holder. The oily blue cloud finally works to his advantage as he pulls away, the gas jockey unable to see the licence plate through the smoke screen.

A LITTLE OVER A YEAR ago, while travelling from one grad party to another, Kevin McCullough leaned out the window and got a face full of post. Alcohol was involved. That was the beginning of a safe grad campaign that was in force by the time Gibson walked onstage to receive his paper tube and shake a series of designated hands.

The grad party was something that pleased both the teachers and the parents. That was important because they almost outnumbered the grads. They covered the entire east side of the gym, staring down fun wherever they saw it, eager to prevent kids from doing what they'd done when they were younger. Even the washroom was no refuge, as Mr. Pinkney, some beefy hockey dad, included it in his rounds of the building.

Of course, Mr. Pinkney and all of the concerned parents were looking for the drugs and alcohol that were allegedly so commonplace among Gibson's generation. There was no booze allowed, but the kids were free to guzzle all the pop they could handle while a specially approved DJ played music the whole family could enjoy.

In the washroom Gibson heard where the real fun was going to be. While he and his date shuffled around on a darkened basketball court, others were hauling firewood down to the beach. By the time the good clean fun was wrapping up and decent children were saying their good-byes, the other party would just be starting.

The propaganda had finally wormed into Gibson's head. Perhaps staying in the parentally supervised gym ghetto was better than dodging super-fast, runaway sports cars that blasted through intersections at two hundred klicks, kids hanging out the window, throwing beer bottles at the heads of old ladies until the crash, young bodies twitching and broken, eviscerated by metal and glass. Even those who didn't crash and burn would find some other way to drain their alcohol-thinned blood. Because they were teenagers, completely unpredictable and untrustworthy, preprogrammed to self-destruct.

Sheena seemed happy. Two months before grad, she had tracked Gibson down in the library and laid out her proposal.

—I've heard you don't have a date for grad yet.

—That's two months away.

—A lot of people have already made their commitments. Now, I'm willing to be your date, but I don't want to be overshadowed. I refuse to be some boy's accessory. If you're willing to cooperate, I think this can work out for both of us. It might even be fun.

She was her own person, she went on to clarify, though no one had ever thought otherwise. Even from a distance you could tell that no one would casually lay their hands on her life. Even so, she kept laying down boundaries until Gibson felt he had been penned into a box. A tiny part of her evening with a tiny role to play. There would be no sex before, during, or after the party. Any rumours he started about this would be dealt with quickly and severely. She also had to be free to leave him for short periods to visit with her friends. Their handshake had the finality of a signed contract. She looked beyond him, or through him, to her future— a seamless transition between school and university, a full scholarship in computer science.

It didn't mean anything, but that had been okay by Gibson.

His whole year had been full of things that didn't mean anything. And it was true that their arrangement had eliminated the task of finding a real date, that is, a girl who liked him.

His friends were surprised and impressed with his date. Gibson guessed he gave the appearance of someone who was having fun. He knew if he could look outside he'd see the faint glow of the pagan fires on the lake, a fire pit on the shore, or someone's parents' cabin, parents who'd had the grace to be somewhere else on that night.

They were swaying to Enya when Gibson pulled Sheena closer than the agreed-upon six-inch limit. It wasn't sexual, he just wanted to be closer to her ear.

—I don't think anyone else is feeling the way I am tonight.

—What are you talking about?

—We missed something by doing it this way. Do you know what I mean?

—No, I don't.

—Well, I have to go then.

He didn't head toward the lake, or attempt to find his imagined parties, but he felt better outside, walking down a dark street in a quiet neighbourhood.

Soon after Gibson enters Kitsilano, a Land Rover pulls up to him at an intersection and the passenger starts screaming at him, pointing to the back of his car. Her face—probably quite beautiful in a relaxed state—is now contorted with anger. Even her pompom of a dog is snarling, its spit dripping down onto the leather upholstery. He pretends not to speak English, holding his hands up in the air and trying to look puzzled.

People on the sidewalk are staring at him. Farther down 4th Avenue, he feels as though he's driving through a gauntlet of shiny stores and beautiful people that he's offended with his smelly, noisy, leaky bomb of a car. He knows he's contaminating their streets, their sewers, their precious air. He knows it's bad, but he has to get to the beach.

ONE NIGHT HE HAD ONE dance with one girl. That's what he remembers from his visit to Vancouver last summer. He didn't want to go to Synergy. As he explained to his friend Jeff, he didn't like dance clubs, smoke, drinking, or shouting to be heard. Jeff promised him a game of pool but pulled him into the bar at the last moment. Gibson didn't care that it was so cool it didn't advertise, so cool you couldn't even tell it was a club from outside. Jeff wanted to join up with someone he'd met at Bar None the night before. The moment they entered, Jeff disappeared, darting between tight clumps of people, into the smoky haze.

Gibson found an opening on the rail next to the dance floor. The couple on his left headed out to dance, and moments later their spot was filled. He felt someone brush his elbow. She was close to him but turned away, talking to her friend. The gentle nudging game continued until she smiled at him as he turned in her direction. A slow song came on and she took his hand. Close to her warmth she smelled sweet, her perfume something tropical. He swayed with her and imagined how she'd taste. He told her she had a nice body, and she said she was sure he had the same. Gibson's hand went lower on her back and then she kissed him. He didn't even know her name, but everything was already shifting.

Jeff tapped Gibson's shoulder. The small group he had attracted felt it was really important to go to Richard's on Richards, because somebody knew the brother of someone in the band and the backstage parties were legendary. As Jeff pulled him away, Gibson reached back for the woman and she leaned forward and shouted into his ear.

—I live in Kitsilano, close to the beach.

—Okay, but what's your phone number?

She smiled and waved and as Gibson was being pulled away, some other guy was already moving in. She watched his departure, then turned to face the new man.

At Richard's on Richards, Gibson pouted on his bar stool while Jeff's group moved around him. He could go back to Synergy but he knew enough about bar dynamics to know that if he did, it would be completely different. She would be gone, or worse, some guy would have his tongue down her throat. When he pulled out a crumpled ball of bills to pay for his beer, he noticed a small strip of paper. It was Razi's phone number. Her name was Razi.

WHEN HIS CAR BEGINS TO sputter Gibson thinks a whiff of the ocean air has overwhelmed it. It finally dies with a block to go, out of gas. He rolls to a stop, bumping against the curb. Behind him, the seizure-inducing strobe lights of a police car. He'd like to take this seriously but it's hard to feel anything more than fatigue.

Gibson stares at the belt full of gadgets while the cop looks at the licence and registration and rambles on about the complaints. Local residents are upset about a red car of this make spewing blue smoke and spilling gas on the road. His partner gets on his knees to check for a leak but finds nothing. They want to verify the exhaust pipe discharge, but despite ten seconds of cranking, Gibson's car will not start.

Gibson points to the cooler as the most likely source of the "leak." When the ice melted, the water leaked out through the drainage cap onto the rug, through rusted holes, then onto the road. The police seem satisfied and happy to clear up the misunderstanding in a way that will not involve paperwork. They have responded to a concern, stopped a suspect, investigated complaints, and now it's time to move on. Gibson stares at the cracked section of curb between his feet. The fender takes his weight without falling off. The police car, back to drab running lights, rolls slowly away toward some other area of crisis.

He walks down to the beach, toward a group of women playing volleyball. The blonde one fails to block a spike and the ball rolls to him. He picks it up and notices sand sticking to the ball where it glanced against her sweaty arm. He stares at it until the powerfully beautiful player asks for the ball. She gives him an amused once-over and he wonders what she must think of him, but it doesn't really matter. Razi lives nearby. She'll take him in and kiss him, or she'll take a peek through the peephole and wait for him to leave, or she'll look dumbly at the shabby-looking stranger on her doorstep. She owes him nothing, having taken him this far.

Gibson takes his socks and shoes off and works his feet into the sand. He watches the game, propped up on his elbows. He wills the blonde to turn so he can see her face again, beaming the command through the back of her head. She leaps up, arches her back, and spikes the ball just inside the line. She turns then, but only to check if someone, anyone, has seen it.

BREAKING ON THE WHEEL

AT NIGHT DANA CAN SEE WINNIPEG FROM the top of the Ferris wheel, not the actual buildings but light reflected off a ceiling of clouds. During the day she can see for miles, and each time she reaches the top, she strains to delay her descent toward the mediocrity of ground level, the gas station, her father standing at the controls, yelling at her to smile.

Smiling is important, because if people see her smiling and realize how much fun it is, everyone will want to take a ride. Dana is the only one riding, just like yesterday and the day before. When this thing gets going she can give up her seat to a paying customer. She doesn't mind helping, but she wonders how long it will be before people realize how much fun it is.

There's a brown crust of burned corn forming on the bottom of the pot. Dana can't smell it, but she knows she forgot to turn the heat down before she came out to help her father. It would take two minutes to run back to the house, turn it down, and run back, but Bob's not interested.

—Let it burn. We have a business to run.

She's slung to the top again, while her mother sits in the kitchen, every curtain in the house drawn closed.

On Saturday, a silver BMW came in for gas and an oil check. The mother seemed so uncomfortable touching anything that was dirty or had the potential to be dirty that Bob did it all for her, even though his was a self-serve station. Her child shyly approached the Ferris wheel and Dana could tell, even from a distance, that the girl was about her age. If she had been on the ground, she might have been able to make a new friend.

Her tank full, the mother went to retrieve her child with Bob close behind. She looked at the wheel the same way she had looked at the gas pump: dirty or potentially dirty. Bob noticed the sharp crease in her pants and thought how strange it was that some clothes looked expensive and others didn't, even though they were often made of the same stuff.

—Five bucks.

The mother was startled. She grabbed her girl by the shoulder and directed her toward the car.

—No, two fifty. Five bucks for you and the kid.

He stood directly between them and the car, his body stiff, but did not pursue her when she guided her child around him. From her seat, Dana saw them group together briefly, then split apart. The girl glanced back at Dana, following the circle she cut in the air.

Bob thought he knew what he needed to know about business, but over the past eight months he's been learning a whole lot more. Most people would rather pull over for gas at the intersection of 332 and the Trans-Canada. Most people would rather do that than turn right on a service-road exit and follow that for half a mile until they got to Bob Hascall's gas station, locally owned and operated. They'd rather go to the Esso and duck into Tim Hortons to get a couple of maple-dipped donuts, or maybe a soup and sandwich, on their way to hell and gone.

The Esso hasn't been there long, but it sure has been a punch in the guts for Bob. He's taken to advertising as a way of regaining lost business. There's a spray-painted banner that reads CHEAP GAS on a plywood sheet, propped up in the ditch just before the turnoff. For the past three weeks, just after closing, he's been edging the sign closer to the road. It's halfway into the shoulder now, almost close enough to make contact with traffic. Below CHEAP GAS, in slightly smaller letters, Bob has added FUN FARE.

ON SUNDAY, A GREEN VAN skidded to a stop and when the sliding door opened, a bunch of teenagers jumped out. They were dressed in shorts, and Dana could see an inflated inner tube in the back along with a couple of coolers. Lake Winnipeg, she guessed, or maybe a party on the riverbank.

The loud one, red-haired and skinny, was chasing the fat one with a can that squirted dry chemical goo. The driver blasted the horn while the two were in front, wrestling for control of the can. It looked like the same kind of fun promised in beer commercials. Not everyone was beautiful, but there was a lot of laughing and screaming and everyone was in on it. The skinny one became winded from his pursuit and bent over with his hands on his knees, gasping for air. In a sideways glance he caught sight of Dana on her metal bench. She was smiling as instructed but he didn't smile back. He shielded his eyes with his hand to see her more clearly. Her smile was now on maximum voltage, her teeth hurting from the pressure, her cheeks beginning to ache.

Silently she was thinking, FUN, FUN, FUN, FUN, hoping the kids would pick up her vibe. Everyone looked at her and fell silent. The sight of her had broken their fun. Dana smiled harder. One of the girls tugged the arm of the skinny one, who eventually turned back to the van. As they drove away, Dana looked down between her feet and felt slightly ill. She had power but it was a horrible power, the power to drive people away. She wished the mounts of the wheel would break so she could roll out of the yard, over the road, into the wheat field, the wheel acting like a giant swather, stalks of grain pulled up and sent flying.

THE CORN BURNS WHILE DORIS sits at the table in a darkened kitchen, using up oxygen, taking up space, being crushed by the weight of everyday events. She scrapes together the strength to stand, walks over to the cupboard and grabs two cans, two possible directions for dessert: a can of peaches or a can of pineapple. Peaches or pineapple. Peaches are nice. Pineapple is also nice. They're both nice. They're both in cans. And the cans are the same size.

The horrid smell of the corn is noted but not connected to herself or any action she might take. After lunch Dana used "supper" as many times as she could in her monologue to Doris, hoping her mother would not try to serve Rice Krispies again.

The old Mom is held in the yellow plastic recipe box. When Dana wants to visit her mother as she used to be, she reads the notes written next to recipes: "Double this if Bill is coming over!!" or "Don't serve if Susan is coming. She can't digest raw cucumbers!" Every comment came with a joy that could not be expressed in mere words. Exclamation marks and smiley faces marked every instance of superfluous glee.

IT ARRIVED ON THE BACK of a flatbed truck. Someone was going to throw it away. Bob thought throwing away working machinery was like throwing away money. Some low-life operator couldn't make a go of it, but being a lowlife, he probably lacked the necessary work ethic.

The driver paused after he had laid down the last beam and secured the hiab on the back of his truck. The area where the picnic bench used to be was covered in metal frames and girders.

—You want some help putting this thing together? I've got a buddy who's done stuff like this a couple of times before.

—No. You've been paid. You can go.

After the driver left, Bob explained to Dana that organization was the key to success in any project. They spent hours flipping beams end for end, looking at the joints, rearranging the frames, before he located a good starting point. By that time Dana's school shirt had a band of grease smeared across it, but luckily Bob was focused on other things.

The first joint turned out to be "sticky." Bob started with a socket wrench and some Liquid Wrench, noodling around for almost half an hour, spraying the joint, testing it with the wrench. He sent Dana for the vise grip and a pry bar. Later he asked for the sledgehammer. He hammered on the pin while Dana held it straight, using all her strength, the vibrations from each blow working their way through her hands, to her elbows and shoulders.

The scientific method finally blew apart and he began to rage on the joint, beating it to death with the sledge. Sparks flew off the metal as Dana backed away from Bob's sweat and swears. All she wanted to do was go back inside, away from him, away from the mosquitoes that seemed to be frenzied by his heavy breathing. Toward nine p.m. she thought she could edge away, back to the comfort of the house in time for *Buffy the Vampire Slayer*, but he spotted her going AWOL and ordered her back, if only to be witness to his misery.

A full night's sleep didn't make him any smarter. He needed Bill.

THEY TAKE THEIR FIRST CUSTOMERS on Monday. The boy's out of the pickup before it stops. His grandfather trails behind. He runs to Bob's side and watches Dana go round and round. Bob, sensing a sale, pushes the throttle down on the coughing engine, and a trail of black smoke comes out the stack. The wheel is now turning at top speed. Grandpa returns to the truck and wipes splattered bugs from the windshield with a very dirty squeegee, expecting the boy to follow, but sometimes it's easier to give in to the child's demands, and how could he not, after seeing the boy's face.

They ride in the car just ahead of Dana. After a couple of turns the boy looks back, and once he has started he can't stop. She smiles at the back of his head, ready for the next chance to show him how much fun she is having. Her power takes away a little joy every time he turns around. First he looks uncertain, then concerned. After a few more turns he looks like he is going to cry. Grandpa doesn't notice the boy's rigid grip on the handlebar. Bob props his cheeks up with his index fingers to remind Dana, but it's too late for charms. Her power has broken the boy. They'll soon go, and they won't be back.

BILL CAME OVER THE MORNING after Bob's tantrum. It was early, before Dana had even started breakfast, and she came out to greet him. There was still dew on the grass, but the birds had been singing for hours. He smiled and put his hand on her shoulder as they walked around the pile of beams and girders. She showed him the joint that had finished off Bob's patience. Bill clucked his disapproval as his fingers traced over stripped threads, dents, bright metal exposed where paint had chipped off. He winced at the bent struts that led to the hub. His voice was only loud enough to be heard above the birds. She leaned closer to catch every soft word.

Bill coaxed and jiggled, welded and greased until the thing started to take shape. Bob came out after breakfast and they worked silently until they ran out of sun. They stopped briefly for the food trays Dana brought, then continued working by the headlights of Bill's truck.

The next morning, Bob tied one of the stays to his trailer hook and slowly pulled the thing up. He left the truck in park and walked to where Bill was adjusting the far stay.

—You can go now, Bill.

—Why don't I stick around until we're sure she runs?

—You're not getting a cut. Just 'cause you helped put a few joints together doesn't mean you're entitled to anything.

—I don't ...

—Don't think you're going to worm in on my business. I knew you were going to pull something like this. Just go.

Bill shook his head as he hefted his tools and his welder into the back of the truck. He winked at Dana and cocked his head for her to follow. He had something for her in the glove compartment.

—And don't be giving her any more stuff. She has enough stuff.

Bill wheeled around and nodded to Bob while he held his cupped hand behind his back. Dana took the carved wooden bird and slipped it into her pocket before her father could approach. Bill drove off and winked at Dana as she waved.

THE MAN WHO STARED AT her on Tuesday had a careful, deliberate manner. He grasped the nozzle firmly, grounded the metal against the edge of the fill pipe and pushed it in slowly until the rubber spill stopper was snug. He noticed Dana as the tank filled, and after he paid Bob he walked to the foot of the wheel to watch her. She smiled but thought it was doomed. Why would a grown man want to go on a Ferris wheel? She smiled anyway. She wondered if she was too ugly to make other people smile. Why else would no one smile back when they looked up at her, having so much fun, all through the skin-frying day and into the mosquito-ridden night?

When she was close to the ground he mouthed the words, Are you okay? She nodded enthusiastically. It seemed possible that her classmates were enduring hellish summers of their own, shovelling mountains of pig manure or stringing barbed wire along fence posts. Possible but not likely. She wanted him to go so he could remember her as the fun-loving smiling girl. She wanted him to go because she couldn't hold back the tears much longer.

LIGHTNING STRIKES AND SHE COUNTS off the miles. Six, seven, eight, nine . . . it's still a long way off. After an hour of watching the sky grow dark, her father will no longer be able to ignore the storm. In the next two turns or so, the wheel will slow and he will let her off. By the end of five turns, that will be it. Ten turns. Twenty-five turns and another lightning strike, six seconds away. At forty-seven turns her count drifts off, but then the wheel slows and stops just short of the point where she can easily get off. Bob runs to the house and comes back with her clear plastic rain cape. He throws it up to her and starts up the wheel again.

Hard rain turns to hail. The engine cuts out, runs for a bit, then dies completely. Bob runs to the station for a bucket of diesel. Inevitably, the wheel stops with Dana at the highest point.

Without the noise and vibration from the engine, she can feel the whole thing twist in the gusts. Rickety. The stays look thin as they go tight then slack with the wind. She considers two deaths: one quick and hot, the other involving a friend from school seeing this.

If she could scream loud enough, maybe Mom would get off the chair. Maybe she'd make the trip a hundred miles from the chair to the window to lift her hundred-pound arms and part the curtain. The sight of her girl on a giant lightning magnet might compel her to grab a coat from the hook and come outside to scream at Bob. Would he listen to her? Would he see her? Would he even understand what was wrong?

Dana closes her eyes. She knows she wouldn't see or hear the strike, but she would see the charge leader, the tiny but inevitable prelude to a strike. Her head bowed, the hood of the raincoat sticks to the clammy skin on the back of her neck.

ILONA LAYS THE MAP ON the hood of the car, using her forearms to pin it down against the wind. The ground is still wet but she's glad; the farmers could use the rain. Dark clouds clear as fast as they came on, and the sun picks up where it left off. Bob Hascall's Gas Bar is the only address given. She wonders if the house is part of the gas station or located nearby.

The man who called from the pay phone told her a confusing story about an amusement park ride but wouldn't leave his name. She doesn't like starting files on the basis of anonymous sources calling from pay phones. Raymond is silent on the passenger's side. He's not what she'd call athletic, but he's a two-hundred-pound guy. He'll do.

Ilona does not like dealing with suspicion and fear. Or standing at the screen door and waiting for someone to come. Ilona does not like the way farms always have a range of lethal weapons at hand. She thinks of a single rifle bullet popping through the aluminum frame of the screen door, entering her liquid-filled guts, deforming into a mushroom shape, then splattering out her back and into Raymond. But mostly, Ilona does not like the way her vision is obscured by the screen door, looking into the dark room behind it, straining to see what's there.

CAPTURE AND RELEASE

ON MONDAY MORNING A HOBO STANDS at the bottom of the driveway. He says something as Mike's Lexus lumbers slowly down from the house on the hill. On Tuesday the hobo is there again. Mike rolls the window down an inch to hear the hobo say, Hey Shithead. The hobo does not touch or pursue the car. Mike doesn't look back until he gets to the stop sign at Arbutus Road. He angles the mirror to take in his drive but can't see what must be the only hobo in Ten Mile Point. He imagines a capture-and-release program involving a barrel trap and a ham sandwich for bait. The hobo would be released onto the Yates Street sidewalk to be among its kind.

Mike's house, set on the rocks high above the town in rarefied air, presents the outward appearance of success. Every week, one or two birds are fooled by a wall of glass as wide as the sky. Its blended architecture yields to rock outcrops instead of displacing them, the exterior matching the greyish-green tones of lichen, the red-brown hue of the Arbutus tree. The real-estate agent claimed it was the highest property in Victoria, and for weeks after they moved in, Mike would amuse Maria by proudly proclaiming that there was no one above them. In the mornings, deer nibble at the gardener's carefully managed vegetation. Mountain mist hangs in air so clean it causes hunger. The ocean is always calm from this distance, and on a sunny day you can see Mount Baker.

Wednesday, same thing: Shithead. During the day, the hobo works his way into Mike's thoughts: I should sell Headman before they announce their results. Where did the hobo come from? Marissa probably hasn't executed that order yet. Has she broken up with another boyfriend? Is that why she's so pissy and forgetful? Her ass looks great in that skirt. When will the hobo go away? Why me?

At the door of their bedroom Mike watches Maria try to find a pair of underwear. She has arranged her boxes in a semicircle, everything within reach, but sometimes her labels betray her. He wishes she would unpack. It would be cute, something they could laugh about if it weren't their fourth month in the place.

Mike has lost weight since the move. He'll be working in his office and remember that he left his phone in the bedroom. That's upstairs, through the main living area and down the hallway to the east end. If his day planner is in the kitchen, that's another hike. Now where's his phone? It's like a bad joke. Yesterday he stumbled into a room he had forgotten. Lose your car keys and it's time to launch an expedition.

Mike rushes downstairs to greet Maria at the door, eager to share his news.

—I made $23,000 in thirty-two minutes.

Maria sighs, takes off her white hospital shoes and begins to massage her feet.

—Gold star, Mikey.

—Everyone thought it would go one way. I knew it wouldn't.

—Good for you.

Maria spends the evening on the phone with her sister, shutting the door to the bedroom when Mike walks by on his way to the west end. He watches a movie on TV, a thriller with lots of plot twists, too many for him to follow.

He's put it off as long as he can, but it's time for Mike to drive in circles again, riding the ring around UVic, in search of his father. Last time, he caught him scrambling over the edge of a dumpster. The time before, he was sitting on the steps of Phoenix Theatre, chatting with people lining up for a show. The maintenance worker, changing a light in one of the lamps, doesn't know what Mike's talking about. Must be new. A clerk at the library is more helpful, directing Mike to the copiers. His father's smell lingers, but he is not there. Mike hovers over an artsy-looking kid with thick-framed glasses.

—Have you seen a stinky hobo guy around here?

—Do you mean Professor Lensky? I saw him near the Engineering building. And by the way, we don't refer to him as the stinky hobo guy.

After a few more directions Mike finds him by the Sedgewick Building. The shopping cart looks new but everything else is the same. The library on wheels is half full of photocopied articles, his own from twenty years ago and those of his contemporaries.

There is no sign of the golf umbrella Mike gave him last month. Or the rain jacket, sweater, emergency cell phone. All those useful gifts are gone, but see if you can get him to part with that Javex bottle. Mike tries to guess if he drinks from it or pisses into it. He still wears that reeking shredded poncho Mike has been trying to replace.

A blonde teenager parts with her boyfriend long enough to leave a muffin on a napkin in front of Mike's father. The old man picks away at it, relaxed, entitled.

—They bring me things. I'm like a squirrel in the park. You can gauge their generosity by the size of my gut.

—I bring you things all the time.

—Did you see the way she looked at you, like you were a cop or a lawyer?

—Next to you I look like a head of state.

—Yeah, think of all the child labourers who suffered so you can feel superior to me.

—This suit was made in Canada.

—Where was the fabric made? Where was the silk and cotton harvested? By whom? Under what conditions?

—I'm sure that wows your muffin-bearers, but you can spare me the commie propaganda.

The professor goes back to his wrinkled, water-stained articles. Mike pulls out a fat roll of hundreds and presses it into the old man's hand. Warmth spreads inside his chest as he walks away, until something hits him in the back of the head. His father has gone back to reading, and the roll sits there in the damp grass. It would feel good to leave it there, have the groundskeep shred it with his mower blades, have a bird rip off bits for its nest, have the next muffin-bearer pay off part of her student loan. Mike covers the distance between them, crouches and pulls his father close.

—Listen, you smelly old fuck. I made $23,000 in thirty-two minutes today. How much did you make? Hey? How much did you make?

The old man's shock fades and he begins to laugh. Mike backs away and picks up his roll. Let muffins sustaineth he who hath rejected the love of his only son. Mike grabs another young lovely's arm as she appears, ready to make an offering of a personal-sized pizza.

—Stay away from the old man. He has rabies.

On Thursday the hobo says, Looking good. Mike was ready for Hey Shithead, even expecting it, and now this. The hobo must be camping out nearby. The surrounding woods, such a great selling feature, now seem menacing. He is camping in there somewhere, possibly spying on them, possibly taking in every detail of their domestic lives.

The next morning, Mike takes extra time setting out his clothes. Three ties are considered and rejected for the new suit, but at least he's settled on the shoes. Maria watches him in the bathroom mirror as he stands, paralyzed by the choices.

—Meeting an important client today?

—Uh, yeah. What do you think of this tie with that shirt?

—That goes fine.

—Wouldn't the blue one be better?

—You wanted my opinion, right?

Mike leaves his topcoat open so the shirt and tie are clearly visible. He rolls the window halfway down as he approaches the hobo. Hey, Shithead. He pounds the wheel and swears as he pulls out onto Arbutus.

Mike stands between Maria and the television.

—You're blocking the view.

She shuts off the TV and flings the remote to the opposite side of the couch. Mike rips a piece of paper in half and gives one piece to Maria, along with a pen.

—You're making me nervous, Mike. What is this for?

—I want you to write down something nice about me, and I'll write something nice about you.

—What do you mean? What kind of thing?

—Can you think of any reason we're together other than convenience and inertia?

—Can we do this some other time?

—No. Just think about it. Would life without me be better or worse?

—What have you been reading?

—Just write.

Maria pulls a coffee-table book onto her lap and sets the paper on top of it. She doodles in the upper left-hand corner. She writes number one and then makes a series of ornate enhancements to it. The tiny hole she began with her pen is enlarged until she can put the paper to her face and see Mike through the peephole, scowling at her. Mike boldly writes numbers one through ten in the margin. Maria does not appear to be taking this seriously.

—How's it going?

She snaps back to attention.

—Fine. And you?

—I'm thinking about it.

—Yeah, me too.

The sun is hot on his neck. He stands to shut the venetian blinds. They clack against the window, startling Maria. A house with a wall of glass seems like a great idea, but only to people who've never owned one. There's a lot to be said for traditional architecture. It's hard to control the temperature in a glass house. On sunny days it's a sauna; at night it's a heat sink.

—How many do you have?

—I've got one.

—Me too.

—What's yours?

—Maria does not intend to hurt me. And you?

—Mike tries very hard.

—Those are pretty pathetic.

—It was your idea.

The hobo is probably within three hundred feet of their house, covered in a stinky blanket or a clear plastic tarp. He may or may not have clear insight into his own actions. It seems a lot to ask of anyone. Neighbours probably pass nearby, take a sharp whiff, and then dismiss it as the rotting carcass of a raccoon or some other woodland creature. The dogs must go nuts, straining against their leashes. Mike imagines a simpler life: survive the night, stand at the end of the drive, call some guy a shithead. It has some appeal.

There might be a certain purity in surviving off turfed food scraps, or root vegetables from backyard gardens.

Maria waits till Mike is almost asleep before pushing into his back steadily with her elbow.

—What is it?

—I don't think we're doing anything wrong, you and I, but I'm not having any fun.

—Fun? We're not kids anymore.

She sighs and rolls over to her side. He waits for her to say something else but soon her breathing is deep. What was the last fun thing he did with Maria? When was the last time he had any kind of fun? It's not the same as satisfaction, enjoyment or a feeling of well-being. Did you have fun? An immediate, honest answer is either yes or no.

2009. Maria and Mike were playing badminton on the beach at the El Cid resort in Mazatlan. They were both very drunk and well on their way to sunburns. Everything that followed on that trip would suck, but at that moment, full up on fruity drinks, chasing after the bird, whacking away at it with cheap rackets that were coming apart, falling on the sand and on each other. That was fun.

Mike hasn't even finished dressing, and already the adrenaline is flowing. There will be no more casual insults at the foot of the drive. He has no plan other than weakly muttering tough-guy lines from bad movies and trying to convince himself that under the right conditions, depending on the other person's self-esteem and general level of fear, in the right light, it might be possible for some other person, of lesser height and weight, to be intimidated by him. As the garage door rises, he grips the wheel, ready, determined. Fog spills down the hill like a gas as he waits for the hobo to appear. He gets out of his car and looks as far as he can in every direction, fully satisfied there is no one there before driving on.

HOW BEAUTIFUL, HOW MOVING

THEY COME AT NIGHT AND ENTER THE house like thieves. They know the history and the value of the items. They know the owner lies dying in the hospital.

LEONA RUSHES INTO BELLA'S ROOM, pushing a gust of perfumed air. Leona is the angel of death. What else could you say about a woman whose mission is to see old fools through their last days and then stand up in church and tell the congregation about it? Edna Cardinal, how beautiful a death, how peaceful. Harold Steiner, with the Creator now. Joseph Fothergill, finding his final resting place. Just as the military has an arsenal of euphemisms for killing, Leona calls death anything but death. The elderly pass away, pass on, slip away, go to a better place, become one with the Maker, or go to be with Jesus. This attractive thirty-seven-year-old will stand up and tell rows and rows of withering crones that death is part of life. Bella knows Joseph Fothergill didn't find his final resting place. He spent his last conscious minutes screaming for the doctor to kill him, even after they had drilled three holes in his head to drain off the fluid. In any case, Leona by your bedside with a smile and flowers is a bad sign on any day of the week.

ROB STANDS IN THE MIDDLE of the living room as Susan darts after porcelain ballet dancers and cats in various playful positions. Veronica tries to get a heavy painting off the wall. Boxes spring to shape and packing paper is ripped off the roll. Rob's feet are shoulder width, his arms up, showing a palm to each sister like a cop trying to stop traffic. He has pleaded with his sisters for an organized, orderly approach, but they've gone straight to looting and pillaging.

Failure to act now will leave him with nothing from his mother's estate. He has to start with something small, the closest thing, a glass candleholder from Sweden that feels heavy in his hands. He wraps it badly and places it on the bottom of a cardboard box with his name written on the side.

Soon he has momentum, launching expeditions to the upper rooms, throwing anything that looks valuable into his box. He can trade some of it later for stuff he really wants, but right now he needs to hoard or he'll lose his stake.

BELLA HAS COME TO UNDERSTAND the widely misunderstood concept of the hospital visit. People who don't really want to be there guilt themselves into staying longer than they should, when she doesn't even want to see them. Some would rather hide than visit, hoping that death is just a popular plot device. Others make short calls to her room early in the morning with detailed lists of the obstacles preventing them from visiting today, but they'll come; they'll come as soon as they can.

As a service to others, she considers writing a pamphlet that could be printed and stacked with other public-health notices near Admitting. She would call it "Your First Hospital Visit." Her suggestions would be simple: If you don't want to come, don't. If you do come, don't stay too long. Don't say stupid things. Think about what you're going to say before you say it. Don't say it's something we all have to face. Don't ask someone if they've made their peace. Don't stare with a pained expression as if watching a boring and sad television show that only gets interesting toward the end, with a close shot on the death rattle, the slight change in the angle of the head on the pillow as life leaves the body.

Bella alternates her gaze between the muted TV and the definitely-not-muted Leona, a self-appointed hope dispenser who attempts to cheer up Bella by describing her latest trip to Paris. The whole congregation tracks Leona's husband's promotions by the way she dresses on Sunday mornings and their vacations, which have progressed from a week in a bed-and-breakfast near Stonehenge, to a four-week bird-watching tour in Costa Rica, to a month and a half on an Antarctic cruise. She is also the woman of a thousand hats, some large, some disk-like, some flouffy and ruffled, each one attached to a charming story: a tiny shop in Munich that was just about to close, the merchant in Hong Kong who haggled with her for almost half an hour. Today, instead of some exotic flying saucer that would take up half the room, she wears a small navy-blue thing, not at all overpowering or flamboyant, perfect for visiting the terminally ill.

Bella hates her room. It seems tired and worn from the lives that have passed through, the pain held in its walls. Lying on the thin sheets of a beaten-up hospital bed, flashed with scenes of junk TV, is not a dignified way to pass from one realm to another. Today's viewing included a show about a couple whose seven adult children all refused to leave home. There were a lot of talk shows hosted by people who were not very good at talking or listening, only good at being stars.

She fantasizes a renovation where the bed would be widened, covered with a duvet and positioned to face an enlarged window. All wires, tubes and machines would be removed and replaced with plants. The current setup, a technologized pen designed for the convenience of the body mechanics, would be covered with fresh rich paint, Navajo red maybe, anything but the current institutional mint.

BOTH SISTERS GRAB THE VASE that sits on the mantle over the fireplace. Both smile at each other as they get a better grip on the thing. Susan was the one who gave it to Mother. But Veronica gave Susan a loan to pay for it, a loan which has not been repaid. Robert, coming down the stairs with his box heaped full, also made a contribution to the vase fund that Christmas. Eventually they agree to put it in a box marked "Contentious Claims."

Rob looks closely at two serviette holders he found in a cabinet in the practically untouched dining room.

—It's real silver.

Both women rush toward him. Veronica's elbow knocks a lamp to the floor. The screaming starts just as the last rounded fragment has stopped rocking. Yes, it was Veronica's elbow that knocked it off, but Susan was the one who tried to push past her. Robert quietly slips the holders into his pocket and moves on to the kitchen. It's probably safer that way.

BELLA CAME IN TWO WEEKS ago with a bad fever and a cough. She was scared enough to bring her will and a list of relatives she thought she should call. Dr. Phibbs was puzzled and the testing was endless. She lost her appetite and couldn't keep anything down. Within five days they were considering feeding her intravenously. The emphasis of the doctor's brief chats changed from fixing her to making her comfortable.

She went along with the dying to meet expectations. The children were already on their way. She was about the right age for it. Sixty-seven seemed a bit young, but no one was too surprised. There was nothing else to do but get on with it. Her bed should be used by someone who might recover. She was a drain on everyone's resources. She didn't want to be like an employee who announces she's leaving, attends a big farewell party and then decides to stay.

When her children come to visit, they file in with sad faces and pile small useless gifts on her bed until they spill onto the floor. She wishes they would spend more time with her now that they're here, a few minutes from the hospital, in a city where they have no business and few friends, but they've trained her not to question their busy lives. The efficient daily visit enables them to fulfill their obligations to their dying mother by offering things. It's her obligation to decline these things.

Leona begins to wrap up the visit in a rising tone. In summary, have faith and try to eat. Bella doesn't tell her that she's been eating like an animal, just not the death cookies that Leona brings over.

POLICY FORMS QUICKLY AND NEW rules are shouted back and forth between the children, who spread through the house, mining every cupboard and drawer. The giver of a gift to Mother has the right to take back that gift. Susan cedes all claims to flatware in exchange for all the linen, including the crocheted tablecloths. And finally, worried about the big boxes Rob keeps hauling downstairs, Susan insists that packing should proceed one room at a time with all present.

ON THE MORNING OF THE sixth day, Bella awoke confused by her condition. Her cough was gone and when lunch arrived, she looked down at the inoffensive vegetable soup with its pack of plastic-sealed crackers ready at the side, and it looked good to her. It tasted even better. It wasn't possible to keep the dirty secret of her health for very long. Nurses and doctors checked, then rechecked her chart. She heard quiet conversations in her doorway, murmured measurements and acronyms, the names of drugs no longer required.

Now she fiddles with the wrapping on a ham-and-cheese

sandwich, squishing against the sides of the plastic container, making it crackle. The seal ruptures and she holds it to her nose. She draws in the moisture and the tangy smell—mayonnaise mixed with mustard? She peels back the tinfoil cover on the chocolate pudding and spoons in a great dollop of it, forcing it from one cheek to the other, swooshing it around her mouth. Leona's tiny gift basket falls to the floor as Bella moves up in her bed, sitting higher to keep the food off her gown. She likes to eat during the nature show, ripping apart her ham sandwich the same way wolves rip flesh off a deer.

SOMEONE SHOULD GO TO THE hospital. But who should it be, and how can the others be trusted not to continue? They usually go together, so it isn't really anyone's turn. But someone should go. It would take awhile to get ready, and by then it would be close to 7:30 p.m., and visiting hours are over at 8:00. Is it really worth it? The siblings all seem to agree. Tomorrow would be better.

DR. PHIBBS TELLS BELLA THAT she'll be sleeping in her own bed tonight. It feels like some sort of graduation. The children won't be happy with this false alarm. Susan was in pre-trial preparation for her firm's most important client when she received Bella's call. Veronica came all the way from Nova Scotia, leaving her husband behind to care for two flu-stricken children. She can't bring herself to call them, and the hospital won't let her take a cab home alone. Someone has to pick her up.

She looks through her suddenly sparse address book. X

through Z have no entries, and many other addresses are for dead people she can't cross out. She has Leona's number from their time together on the fundraising committee, but Bella's stubborn insistence on survival would confuse the poor woman. Leona is probably thinking ahead to Sunday's announcement: Bella's passing, how beautiful, how moving.

Ed Schmidt would read something into it if she called him. It would be awkward and embarrassing. He seemed so kind and gentle with her, offering his support even as the soil was being shovelled onto Jake's coffin. She enjoyed going with him to choir practice, but he had to ruin it with his grand proposal, deflating Bella's thoughts of simple friendship.

Verna Holloway, dead. Bernie Pasternak, dead. Candace Williams, living in Summerland now. She flips through her book again and finds Matt Donner all alone in the Ds. He isn't family. She can't really call him a friend but he's dependable, coming every two weeks to cut the grass, clean out the gutters and do whatever jobs need doing.

—Hello? Is Matt there?

—Ms. Cowper? Yes, he's here but he's working on a school project tonight.

Bella's tempted to say good-bye and hang up.

—I wonder if I could bother . . . Do you think it'd be too much trouble if . . . I'm sorry. I need Matt to pick me up from the hospital.

—Just a moment.

—I'll pay him.

Mrs. Donner doesn't hear that last part. She's already on her way to get Matt. Bella waits for him with her hands folded in her lap, her bag neatly packed. She'll miss looking out onto the snow-covered fields, the silent stream of cars on Pembina Highway ebbing and flowing between downtown and the suburbs, the traffic quiet and peaceful from this distance.

ROBERT HOLDS SOME DOILIES IN the air, out of reach of his two sisters. Susan feigns disinterest until Robert lowers his arm, and then she lunges at him again. He thinks he should have them, considering that his sisters already received their fair share. Susan laughs at him.

—That's because doilies are for girls, Robert. Everybody knows that. She didn't give any to you because she didn't know you were a pansy.

Veronica curses and throws down one of the Folio books she got in trade from Susan.

—She put her name in all of them. Can you believe that? That's just going to kill the resale value.

On her way to the upstairs washroom Susan can't stop herself from taking a sneak preview of her mother's bedroom. The jewellery box doesn't have a false bottom. There's no safe in the closet or under a loose board. But there is a rip in the fabric that covers the underside of the box spring. Quite thin, but big enough for a hand to reach through and touch an envelope.

In the bathroom she fumbles with the zipper of her purse. It won't close easily with the cash crammed inside. She persists until she breaks the zipper and one of her nails. She stares at her blushing face in the mirror. Breathe deep, stop smiling, look normal. There's probably enough to renovate the kitchen. Or take a vacation somewhere hot. The wad felt very thick and it looked liked mostly hundreds. Maybe she'll be able to do both.

AT FACE VALUE IT'S JUST a ride home, but Matt approaches Bella's bed wary of what else might be involved. Will she want to pay him for this? Will she want to hire him as a part-time caregiver? There are a few graceful ways to decline the offer. Schoolwork is a solid excuse. No one could argue with that. He's still willing to help her, but he prefers the simplicity of yard work. He doesn't mind her watching him from the window but he tries to avoid the inside of her house, usually receiving his pay on the front steps.

Bella snugs down into the quiet warmth of Matt's car. They drive past the St. Vital shopping centre. She notices heavy frost on the windshields of cars, one very cold cat staring back at her with minimal interest, a street-hockey game just as someone scores a goal, the boy's arms shooting up in the air.

Forty-two years ago there was no mall along this street, and their new house backed onto a farmer's field. There was a slough nearby and bushes that lined the river. Often she saw foxes and rabbits from the kitchen window.

Matt opens her door and offers his arm. She notices him as a full-grown man for the first time, so different from the small boy she first instructed years ago. Now she's embarrassed for having bothered him with this.

Forty-two years ago a taxi dropped her here, and she stood at the foot of the driveway with Susan, her first child, fresh from the hospital. Bella's breath hung in the cold morning air. The sky was still dark blue. Jake had turned the heat down to save fuel, and it was freezing inside. She cranked it up right away, worried about her baby. It seemed colder inside than out. She brought out spare blankets, layered them on the bed and pulled in Susan after her, using her arm to keep the blanket off the baby's face. The bed was pregnant, their breath heating the artificial womb.

Someone has swiped her doormat again but never mind, her kids are home, together for the first time in a long time. Every light in the house is on and it cheers her to think of her children in the house again, as it was so many years ago, the noise of games and laughter. Maybe they will stay a few more days, even though the danger has passed.

First Rob then Susan appears at the living-room window. They seem shocked to see her and it makes her proud of her good health, her mysterious recovery. Matt slowly pulls away, tapping the horn. Susan opens the door and stands there dumbly, blocking the way. Bella finally edges her way past Susan into the warm house.

IMAGING MILAN

IT'S TOO EARLY IN OUR RELATIONSHIP
for you to leave Benni with me. I realize this now that you're thousands of kilometres away. I know your postcard was meant to please
me, but it's no comfort thinking of you thinking of me while you're
in Milan. Briefly, I was honoured that you would trust me with
your only child. Were you counting on that?

Perhaps you've never been here because it's more than half an
hour from a large city. As a concerned parent, you might want to
know where I'm housing your daughter. I live on a ridge on Salt
Spring, the largest of the Gulf Islands in the Strait of Georgia.
My house is surrounded by very large, very tall trees, typical of this
province. I'm ignorant of the Latin, or even the common names
for any of this wild, green growth, but that doesn't diminish my
love of this place as my lungs fill with rain-scrubbed forest air on
morning walks.

My nearest neighbour is a three-minute drive away, but he's
not the kind of neighbour you drop in on. I don't know his name,
how he got his money, or if he's married. I do know what the back
end of his yellow Hummer looks like, as it sits in the driveway

most days. He might just as easily be in Milan this weekend. Perhaps you shared a row on the plane.

Forgive me for spying on your daughter from the kitchen as a hunter might scope out a wild cat from a blind. She likes TV, or more specifically, Judge Mathis dealing out pseudo-wisdom. She enjoys the Cheetos, orange powder ground into leather a small price to pay for subduing the beast, but the Coke is ignored, its perfect layer of cold sweat untouched.

—I'm not doing anything.

She must have caught my scent in a draft.

—I noticed you haven't touched your Coke? Can I get you some other drink? Mountain Dew? 7UP?

—No, thanks.

—I also have diet versions of those drinks.

—Why would I want a diet drink?

—No reason. I'm not saying that you should take a diet drink, I mean, it's not that you're—no, I'm not trying to ... Some people drink it even though they don't need to. I mean, no one really needs to. The taste is different. Some people just like the taste. Better than the non-diet version. There's also water. Evian? Perrier?

—I'm not thirsty.

Are you a careful student of your daughter? Do you notice small things? Big things? Did you know that she does not drink water? She hates the taste of it. Can you imagine hating the taste of something that's critical to your survival?

PAST MIDNIGHT I THINK OF the last line of your card again. I wish you were here, a sentiment so cliché it almost breaks out the other side into originality. I wish you were here, too. I know you would constrict every time a gust pounded the sliding doors. Your heart would also pound, but for a different reason. You would hate and fear it. I fear and love it, the invisible burden on these trees, the terminal crack when one of them succumbs. Since you're missing this, I want to describe everything. That's how you like your danger, isn't it? Described by someone else?

I'm on the edge of a cliff in slippers and a robe. Okay, maybe that's a little overdramatic. I'm standing about three metres from a cliff, but it's not sheer; I wouldn't fall straight to the bottom. There would be plenty of thumps and bumps on the way down. Some gusts seem strong enough to blast me off this ledge. My robe billows and flaps like a flag. You know how I'm always talking about being closer to nature? Well, I don't want to get much closer than this.

Even in this sheltered area the ridiculous wind makes wires howl, breaks arms off swaying giants. My house asserts a few small squares of light against black fury. Don't worry. The structure is solid, and it warms me to think of Benni in the guest room, sleeping through this.

NO, I'M SORRY, I'M WRONG. She's awake. I see the sliver of light under the bathroom door.

—Did the storm wake you?

—Leave me alone.

—I'll be in the kitchen making a snack if you want some company.

Why is your child angry with me? Do you tell her about our fights? Please don't. Let's not be two lawyers trying to win over a jury of one.

I watch from the kitchen, hoping to catch her if she comes out quietly. Had I kept Louis, maybe I'd be enjoying a smoked salmon omelette, but no, tonight it's gluey white bread and cheese. As you have said before, having help is great, but then they're always . . . around. Bite after joyless bite, I think about Benni's first nine years, and what follows the next nine, bouncing between pleasure and pain on her own, like the rest of us. I listen through the door.

—It's alright to be afraid of the wind. It frightens me too sometimes.

There's no flushing, no running water, not even drops falling into a hot, calm bath. No crinkle of plastic, no rip of a match, no zipper from a tote bag, no rustling of fabric.

—What's wrong?

—I'll be out in a minute.

The toilet flushes once, then two more times. Is she old enough to be doing drugs? What could she be flushing down the toilet? She comes out of the bathroom with a dark red smear on a wad of Kleenex.

—I'm bleeding to death.

I wish you were here. You could take your daughter by the hand, guide her to a quiet room with soft lighting, and explain that she is not bleeding to death. In fact, the blood coming from between her legs is something that should—believe it or not—please her. But I can't take your daughter's hand.

—I don't want to die.

—You're not going to die.

—How do you know? You don't even know what's wrong with me.

—There's nothing wrong with you.

—I'm dying.

—Stop saying that.

—I'm bleeding from the inside and it won't stop.

—The bleeding will stop in a few days.

—A few days?!? I'll be dead by then.

I take her to the hospital but it's closed for the night, or permanently. I was hoping for a gentle nurse in the emergency ward. Instead, I've got a girl with half a roll of toilet paper stuffed in her pants, begging for her mother who is somewhere in Milan. She wants to see a doctor and the only doctor I can think of right now is Celia, on South Pender Island. Yes, her doctorate is in English, but maybe she has a good bedside manner.

Benni waits in the car while I use a phone at the Co-op to call about a water taxi. Rick is not pleased that I have called after midnight. He says no. I remind him that his ad in the directory says, Anywhere, anytime.

—It's blowing forty out there. No one is going anywhere. And don't bother calling Island Taxi. They're not crazy either.

—What's your regular rate? I'll pay you triple your regular rate.

—Hang on a second.

Rick walks to another part of the house and I can hear him knocking on a door. I only hear the swears between what the other guy is saying. Rick tells him it's triple rate. They discuss borrowing Dennis's boat, which is apparently bigger. Do you like the way I am being assertive on behalf of your child? Rick comes back to me.

—It's not going to be a comfortable ride.

Do you remember the time we sailed to Catalina Island with Don and his friends? This is nothing like that. It's an aluminum workboat, ugly inside and out. I'm on an old school-bus bench, and Benni's reasonably happy on the driver's seat of an old Jeep. The radar display looks like a child's handheld video game. Rick sits behind a tiny wheel and fires up the diesel. He seems very young and uninterested in conversation, but I try anyway over the drumming of the engine.

—This isn't so bad. I don't see what the big fuss is about?

—Wait till we get outside the harbour.

Soon I see bigger, meaner waves at the entrance. It would be nothing to ask him to take us back to the marina. He'd probably be relieved. But no, I stare through the wind at the rollers, spray blown off the tops. Rick shifts in his seat and looks back at me one last time, as if to say, Speak now. I say nothing. The boat moves forward, because the prop is spinning and you can only pull the throttles back so far before you're in neutral.

Slammed sideways by the first big wave, I'm suddenly angry at Rick for taking us into this. Doesn't he know there's a child involved? But maybe he is a child, not used to considering the safety of another. He takes the waves at all kinds of angles, fiddling with the throttles. I try to understand his technique but there's no pattern to his actions; he's learning as we go, at our expense. Tonight is his practicum in bad weather. Waves sneak up on us, rearing violently before smashing their steep faces against the back of the boat. The lights of the marina have disappeared.

With enough money, you can silence better judgement. That's how wannabe mountaineers end up on Everest and how landlubbers end up in Pacific storms.

Rick says he's going to slow the boat to prevent us from diving into the back of a wave. He changes our course and we settle into a new pattern. Now we're lifted up slightly at the back, and then there's a sickening roll as the wave passes underneath. My head is knocked against the window, and the skipper almost comes off his seat. Some water trickles through the door. A mop bucket comes loose from its tie-down, tumbled by sloshing water on the back deck.

Benni seems wide-eyed but calm. What is she thinking? I know you could tell me. Do you think she's losing interest in her old problem as spray covers the boat and visibility is now less than a mile? What would you do if you were here? Is Benni relaxed because she doesn't realize the danger? If you were here, would you summon magical parental powers? Would you stare down the waves, flatten them with your glare? You'd have a plan, wouldn't you? You wouldn't just sit here with your butt cheeks clenched tight. And so, with you in mind, I scream at Rick.

—Where are the life jackets?

—What?

—Where are the life jackets?

—We're fine. We're going to be fine. Only a few more hours to go.

—Where are the life jackets?

He looks at me as if I have insulted him.

—They're in the locker.

—What about flares?

Another look.

—We're not going to need flares.

—Good. But do you have any?

—They're also in the locker.

I'm not going to stare at the greasy fingerprints on the locker door for too long. For now, I'm just going to accept that inside that tiny space there are three life jackets and a bucket of flares, because that's what the kid said. There's no sign on the door, not even a red cross for a first-aid kit. When we drop between the waves, all I can see is streaked water, higher than the boat. Wind sings off sharp edges and antennas as I look past the froth into the black hole where South Pender used to be. Rick tells me the island is blacked out because of downed lines but assures me we're getting closer, pointing out a red smudge on the radar.

I call Celia's number but when my elbow hits the seat, the phone drops to the deck, lighting up a small section of the metal plate. When I stand up, I'm thrown back into my chair. I try again, get on my knees, and slide headfirst into the sharp metal edge of the seat. Celia's there; I hear her faintly through the noise. I talk as loud as I can while shielding myself from the others.

—My girlfriend's daughter is flowering into a woman.

—You deflowered your girlfriend's daughter?

—No, she's flowering into a woman.

—Would you speak English please?

—Womanhood is upon her.

—What does that mean?

—Please stop laughing.

Having arranged our pickup, I can now concentrate fully on vomit-suppressing thoughts. It helps to look at Benni, sitting there as if we're in a paddleboat on a bright, sunny day at the lake. Even Rick looks pale as he turns to warn us that once we're out of the lee of Moresby, it'll be a little rough, but only for the last few miles into Bedwell Harbour.

The waves are farther apart and bigger, faster. On each crest the wind spikes, then lowers again as we drop. Probably just another day on the water for Rick. That shrieking sound? Normal. The pounding that seems to be loosening the rivets of this boat? All normal. I wonder if there's a life raft. Of course there's a life raft. Something really compact, something strong that would fit all of us. Naturally, it's tucked inside the locker, along with the rest of the lifesaving gear. No need to ask. Because it's about trust now, this boat, this kid. I'm trusting.

—Is this normal?

—Yes, this is normal for a strong gale.

—Is there a life raft?

Rick doesn't turn around, so I'm not sure he heard me. He probably heard me. I suppose I could ask again. Celia will meet us at the dock, if and when we get there. Benni reaches over and tugs on the shoulder of my jacket.

—How long are you going to be with my mother?

The fire extinguisher comes loose from its bracket and barely misses Rick's head.

—That's a strange question.

The cribbage board leaps off the shelf, taking Rick's thermos with it. I can hear the tinkle of broken glass inside as it rolls around the deck.

—It would help if you could tell me. Over three months? A year or two?

—Can we talk about this later?

Is our connection strong enough that you feel my relief all the way from Italy as I step off the boat, or will it take years for us to be that close? Rick ties up the boat, opting for a night on Pender rather than a head-on pounding on the way back. It's raining and cold and I don't care. I still feel sick, but I can't stop smiling. I hug Benni, and again, lifting her and squeezing.

The headlights of Celia's Beetle sweep onto the marina lot, the rasp and rattle of the engine faint and mixed with the wind. Behind us, all the wires and masts from the sailboats sing along in an eerie chorus. She takes us off the main road, winding through the dark woods, stopping once to pull away a branch that is blocking the drive. Her old house sits with authority, having earned the right to live among the trees unmolested. In the living room we stand close to the fire, dripping on her carpet. I am unable to stand solidly on my feet, still rocking from the boat while I get used to a living room full of cats, candles, and other comfy things.

—Benni would like to be examined as soon as possible, Doctor.

—Very well, I will examine the patient. You can stay out here in the waiting room and keep the cats company.

—Gladly, Doctor.

While Celia examines Benni in the washroom, calming her with a positive prognosis, I imagine you in Milan. The outfit you put on pinches your left breast, and being in such a damn hurry to put it on and get out there, you do not straighten it out, so you suffer as you stroll down the catwalk, and resentment builds, flowering out from this pinching sensation into general boredom with the show, sour disgust with the whole industry. And to everyone looking at you, your discomfort is irrelevant, as it always is. And you realize all you want to do is cash in your chips and be with me on this island and do something groovy like be a beekeeper or make wind chimes out of seashells and sell them to American tourists down at the market, but then you think about all the money you have spent, about wrinkles that have become more prominent, the years you have left, and curse the long lenses that have swung over like eager penises to point at younger, newer women.

THE JANITOR

CARL DIDN'T KNOW WHY HE LIED. LIED was the wrong word. Carl didn't know why he let the lie happen. The receptionist mistook him for the new principal and he didn't correct her. She babbled on until she created her own explanation: she had marked down the wrong date on her calendar.

Saying nothing was a good way to hide ignorance. Carl clung to that belief no matter how many times it failed him. When he was sixteen he drove seven hours to Fort Mac to make his first and last major buy. He threw up next to a dumpster, entered the back door of an abandoned dry cleaner, and made his way to the storeroom. He sat at the table and waited. The guy walked in, took Carl's bag of money, and walked out. Carl said nothing. He didn't want to look like a bumpkin, unaware of how things were done in the big city, but he had let go of the cash. He sat in a cracked plastic chair that pinched his butt when he moved. He stared at his watch, each blinking second a judgment. He memorized the warning label on an empty pail of cleaner. He was having a staring contest with the skull and crossbones when the guy came back with a fat envelope full of windowpanes.

Ms. Gill came out to the reception area and introduced herself as the one who had been acting principal for the past two months. She was surprised to see him, as she had expected him the next day. When he responded with a shrug, she led him to his new office. She apologized for the small size, and he thought to himself that it was almost big enough for putting practice.

Carl settled into the most amazing sitting experience he had ever had. He didn't need to tilt or slouch to get comfortable. A soft, rounded bulge fit perfectly into his lumbar region. To sit in it was to become one with it. Melissa introduced herself and placed a box of five thousand business cards on his desk. Carl picked up the first one and read the full name of the man whose life he was borrowing: James McGraw, Principal, Lester B. Pearson High School.

Ms. Gill was eager to show off their modern facilities, the chemistry lab, the renovated gym, but most of all she wanted to talk about her new zero-tolerance initiative. A number of undesirables had already been ejected from the student population, making it a safer, happier, more educational place to be. Her PowerPoint slide show had many colourful charts, which seemed to offer proof that life at the school had improved. He tried to follow what she was saying, but the lack of pauses between her words made it impossible. He sensed by her rising tone that the presentation was over, and his mood lightened. She had completely reorganized the personnel files—that was their first stop—but first she wanted his opinion on the use of parent volunteers for extracurricular activities. The subject had been changed, but he was still unable to latch on to more than a word here and there. Her speech became noise, and soon after, he had blocked it out altogether.

They passed a girl who was hanging on tightly to the rail of the stairway. Carl could see she was about to cry. He paused while Ms. Gill continued on, the girl by the rail taking his full attention. He walked back down the stairs and stood behind her.

—What's wrong?

She turned around, startled, and broke down into the kind of full-body crying that most tried to save for the privacy of a bedroom. They stood facing each other while her tears made a mess of her makeup. He pulled her into him and held her. The bell rang and students flooded out into the hallways, rushing past them as they stood unmoving. Some stared, some didn't notice, but no one did or said anything to disturb them. Except Ms. Gill, who began to clear her throat as if she were choking on a rice cake. The girl looked up at Carl.

—Who are you?

—You can call me Jim.

—You're nice, Jim.

She quietly picked up her books and joined the stream of students heading for class. Ms. Gill did not look pleased.

—I didn't want to correct you in front of the student, but please don't touch the students. If a student has emotional or psychological problems, we direct them to the guidance counsellor. Where did you say you worked before you came here?

Carl pretended not to hear the question, merging into the flow, making his way to the ground floor while Ms. Gill struggled to keep up. Fifteen minutes later, a kid in the library passed him and said, Hi Jim. Three others did the same before Carl had made it back to the office. Ms. Gill pointed out that the position of principal was not a popularity contest.

Carl wondered how anyone ever got any work done while sitting in a chair that could easily put you to sleep. Maybe that was the point. Maybe with the door shut, the blinds closed, and the receptionist guarding the door, he'd be able to sleep till noon. Maybe that's what a principal did.

Ms. Gill walked in without knocking and dropped a heavy black binder on the desk in front of him.

—It would no doubt be helpful for you to review minutes from our meetings going back at least six months. It'll give you some idea of how we do things here, what kind of issues we've been dealing with.

They were organized from most recent to oldest, and colour-coded stickers were used to mark memos related to subjects discussed in the minutes. Carl watched her throat bob as she explained the coding system. She had a brooch the shape of a playful kitten, which didn't suit her. He imagined a tomcat brooch, ears back, hissing, and combat ready. There was a strange calm in the room, and Carl looked up to notice she was gone.

Yes, it was all very critical stuff. There was a notice about students who were getting into the staff washroom, and additional clarification regarding payment for monthly parking passes. It was all there, for sure, and it was killing Carl to muck through the first ten pages. He flipped to the middle but it didn't get any better. He found a diversion in the bottom desk drawer. The old principal's calendar was much more interesting than a mountain of memos, and he was sure he'd find the reason for the old man's departure if he looked close enough.

Carl disappeared around eleven a.m. He knew where he was, of course, and didn't seem very concerned that it took Ms. Gill half an hour to find him sweeping the third-floor hallway. He was leaning on his broom, debating with a group of students the claim that Marilyn Manson had a PhD from Harvard.

Ms. Gill hailed him from down the hall, and the group quickly scattered.

—What are you doing?

—Sweeping.

—Our cleaning staff makes regular rounds.

—Floor's dirty now.

—Oh, I see what you're doing. I see what this is. This is supposed to be symbolic, right?

—No, this is supposed to get the floor clean.

—Very clever. Don't let me hold you up.

Carl watched her walk away and tried to figure out what she had been talking about. He considered calling her back to ask her, but silence was safer.

After introductions in the staff lounge, it seemed like the teachers were waiting for him to say something. There was nothing to say. How could there be? He had just arrived. He did his best to get something started.

—Did anyone watch that new show last night? It's the one with the interviews at the start and then the people who were being interviewed put on boxing gloves and duke it out in the ring. I forget the name. It's a stupid name. Sharon, you know the one I'm talking about, right?

—I don't watch television.

—Yeah, and I don't masturbate. Come on, somebody must have heard of this show.

Robert finally spoke.

—*Fiddle Faddle*.

—That's it, *Fiddle Faddle*!

—It's my kid's favourite show. She's eight.

—I seen the star of that show. I seen him when he was in town just standing on the street corner like a regular person.

Everyone stared at Carl. He wondered if there was something hanging off his nose, or a bit of food stuck in his teeth. Sharon smiled painfully and asked him a question.

—Jim, what's your vision for the direction of the school?

—Is the school moving?

—No.

—Well, I guess we don't have to worry about direction then.

—What I meant was . . .

—Hold that thought.

Carl pushed his chair back and walked out. Most of his lunch was finished anyway, and he needed some fresh air. He didn't like sitting with the teachers. They weren't very friendly, and every question seemed to be a trap.

When Carl walked out into the yard, the students behind him noticed. He was headed toward the small group of fringe types that stood like ugly weeds on a manicured lawn. The second- and third-floor landings overlooking the yard soon filled, and on the ground floor kids spilled out onto the trampled grass to watch.

Ms. Gill pushed her way past the others to see Jim headed toward the group. Her fists were clenched. Jim wasn't escorted by a security guard or a police officer. He was walking over as if he were about to say hi to the neighbour over the fence.

Carl walked toward them and they ignored him. He paused for a moment just outside the group, and even from a distance Ms. Gill could see their heads go back in laughter. He took a step forward into their circle and everyone waited. There was no close-quarters takedown. He didn't snatch the joint from the lips of the kid next to him. There were no searches, no confiscation. He just stood there and talked to them as if everything were normal. He turned around as someone in the group pointed back to the school, and he waved at all the expectant faces. Eventually the spectators became bored and shuffled back to their classes.

Ms. Gill's face was still red as she stood on the threshold to Carl's office with a file folder in her hand. He got up from his desk and took it from her grip with some difficulty. When he opened it, he was looking down at his own résumé.

—You'll have to do something about this fellow. He was supposed to be our new janitor, but he didn't show. Could you take care of it?

Carl waited for her to leave, but it became clear that she wanted to see him in action. He called his number and smiled at her until his voicemail kicked in. He told his voicemail, without hesitation, without wavering, that anyone who wanted to work at Lester B. Pearson had to abide by a professional code of conduct. Ms. Gill seemed to light up and nod her head whenever he used a phrase he had read in one of her many memos. He scolded himself for not showing up and said that he expected more of himself. Everyone who worked at this school, from the janitor on up to the principal, was expected to meet or exceed a certain standard. When he had had enough of his own lecture, Carl quietly fired himself and dropped the phone back into its cradle.

—I didn't think you would fire him.

Carl panicked for a second before her memo on the stink-bomb incident in the second-floor washroom came to mind.

—I have zero tolerance for this kind of unacceptable behaviour.

Drawn by noises from the gym, Carl found a game: lights off, no teacher, shirts and skins. They didn't notice him slip in and grab the broom that sat in the corner. He made his way slowly around the court, smiling at the sound of rubber soles chirping against the wooden floor. The skins were taking a beating. Every two points the shirts did a little dance, pointed fingers, taunted the enemy. The skins slouched lower down as they took in the chants. They didn't move as fast, let more passes go, and fought over who was to blame.

Another loose and lazy pass was missed by a skin, and instinctively Carl reached out to stop the ball. The wooden handle of the broom fell on the floor, making a clacking sound that echoed through the gym. He put the ball between his knees and took off his shirt. They laughed until he started to move.

Carl was covered in the sweat of the righteous when Ms. Gill entered the gym with a security guard at her side.

—Put down that ball!

The confused players looked at Ms. Gill then back to Carl. He took a shot from the penalty line. It dinged the rim and a skin sent it back his way. He took five steps back and tried again. He missed the backboard. Five more steps back, he dribbled hard to drown out Ms. Gill.

—PUT DOWN THAT BALL!

Carl pounded the ball into the floor in time with his heart and he saw the ball go down, no backboard, no rim, he saw the ball go down, before it even left his hands.

COMMAND MYSTIQUE

DEAR MA,

It gets hot in Texas, but that ain't nothing compared to the desert. And in Texas I don't have to run around in thirty pounds of gear and body armour. We were hit by a sandstorm today. I saw it coming toward us like a giant tsunami of sand a thousand feet high. When it passed over us it got real dark. If I were the enemy, that's when I would attack. A Black Hawk crashed last week trying to take off in bad visibility. There's no point of reference when the sand is blowing, so the pilots get disoriented. I'm settling in here. It's not too bad but some things suck more than others. I miss your meat loaf. What they call meat loaf here is just a bland clump of mystery meat with a snaky line of ketchup on top for flavour. The food is so gross here, sometimes I skip a meal just so I'll be hungry enough to eat the next. How are things back home? How's Jenny?

DEAR SON,

I was thrilled to get your message this morning. I'm ashamed to say I haven't fully cleaned since your good-bye party. The fire ants have taken full advantage of this. Your cousin says he has a nontoxic cure for them. I know it's silly, but having the party hats and banners around makes me feel closer to you. Your father would be so proud to see you serve your country as he did. I am suffering with you in the heat. Every time my baby suffers, I suffer. I know you don't like it when I call you that, but you will always be my baby. When you get home, I will make as much meat loaf as you can handle. I would send it by mail if that were possible. Things could be worse. Have you been forced to eat any MREs yet? Your father used to call them Meals Ready to Excrete, or Meals Rejected by Ethiopians. Uncle Nick is still in hospital and asks about you often. He is very brave, just like his nephew. Did you know you can attach digital photos to emails? I will send some of Nick on one of his better days.

Dear Ma,

The boys got a good laugh from your email discovery. You can also attach documents and songs. Watch it with the illegal downloads, Ma, or the record company will come after you! Welcome to the Interweb! Things are starting to turn normal around here. It's hard being the new guy when the other guys in my squad are already working well together. Patrols are going okay except that I am having some difficulty orienting myself. The lack of street signs doesn't help, and the buildings all look the same. It's hard for me to lead when I don't know exactly where I am. If the driver was hit, I'd have to rely on someone else to get us back to base. Part of the problem is that I don't pay any attention when I'm not in the driver's seat. We go the same route four or five times and I still don't remember. Getting lost in Austin on the way to Uncle Nick's place is one thing. Over here things are a bit different. Every other day a Humvee comes back with a wound. Sometimes it's just a bullet hole or scorch marks. Other times they come back on a flatbed, still smoking, blown to shit, dripping blood and motor oil. I don't want to add getting lost to our problems.

DEAR SON,

It probably won't make you feel any better to know that your orientation problem is genetic. For years I travelled with your father in the car, chatting away, never noticing where I was going or how I got there. It wasn't until he died that I learned to get around. The easiest way to fix your problem, Son, is to kick that private out of the driver's seat and do it yourself. That will sharpen your attention, especially considering all that is at stake. If you get lost again, start asking the men as if you're quizzing them, stressing the critical importance of directional awareness.

DEAR MA,

Thanks for the tip. I think the guys are impressed that I'm driving. To be honest, the worst job is manning the two-forty with your head poking out the top like a gopher waiting to get his head blown off by Farmer Jim. I've already seen more than I want to here, and I haven't even been shot at yet. Sometimes on patrol I start to hunch over in the foetal position, as if that would protect me from an IED. Maybe it's natural that after seeing this horrible place, some part of me wants to curl up and sneak back into the womb where it's safe, quiet, and peaceful.

DEAR SON,

My womb is closed for business. Sorry to disappoint you. It's alright to say that kind of stuff to me, but don't you EVER say anything like that to the boys. You are a staff sergeant, and the boys need to be reminded of that every day in a hundred different ways. Your father always called it the command mystique. He had it and you better get it, or men will die. They can't believe that you would make a mistake. It goes beyond trust. They've got to genuinely believe that it is impossible for you to make a mistake. Everybody does, of course, but when you do, they have to see something other than a mistake. When you get lost, they see you're taking a different route. When you get fired on unexpectedly, you haven't cluelessly stepped into an ambush—you've drawn out the enemy. When you call in a fire mission on your own position, you are misleading the enemy to think that your squad has been wiped out. What daring! What sacrifice! What a leader!

DEAR MA,

I don't know exactly which John Wayne movies you've been watching, but the reality of war is a little different from the cheerleader version pumped out by Hollywood. Your tip about driving was good, but I'm in a war now, and tips that might be fine for surviving the Texas summer just aren't going to apply out here. You've got to accept that there are things about our situation here that you just don't understand. Out of respect for Dad's experience, I'm going to try the command mystique for a while and see how it goes. I'm not quite sure I can be that Robert Duvall character in *Apocalypse Now* who stands tall and unflinching while bullets

zing past his head. If I can't manage fearless, I am getting better at
never admitting to mistakes, but I'm not sure how well this is going over with the men.

DEAR SON,

I don't think you're getting the command mystique. Don't
doubt anymore. Banish it as an option. None of this is to pump
up your ego. This is survival. If Private stands there in the heat of
it and hesitates for ten seconds in the execution of your order because he has DOUBT about it, those ten seconds could be deadly
for someone else. When God tells you to build an ark, you build
an ark. When Staff tells you to kick down that fucking door, you
kick it down.

DEAR MA,

Did you just use the f-word? Who are you and what have you
done with my mother? You are a bigger hardcase than anyone in
my company. Last night I got an address wrong and I realized it
just as the ram was swinging to break the door down. Instead of
telling the guys, Hang on, I got the wrong house, we just piled in
there and tossed the place. I led the way since I was pretty sure the
occupants weren't a threat, so I came off looking like a gung-ho
commando. You should have seen that family cowering under our
lights. They really thought they were about to be executed. How is
Jenny doing? I've been sending her emails but she hasn't replied.
Could you forward this email to her so she can get my address
right?

Dear Son,

I'm sorry if my tone sounds odd. Now that you're deployed, I feel as though I'm channelling your father. There were many things he could have taught you if he had known you were going to join the Army, but he never thought you would take this path. Not that it matters at this point, but he would not have approved. Yes, I know I said he would be proud to see you serve. Is it possible to think both of those thoughts? I think so. Your father was a complicated man. As far as dear Jenny is concerned, she may just need some time to sort out her own thoughts. This has been a huge adjustment for her.

Dear Ma,

As a squad we are functioning well. Now, if we could only get others to work with us. We have come to rely more and more on close-air support to keep our sector under control. When we get pinned down somewhere, it seems to take the Apaches forever to get to our positions. Sometimes half an hour. I have no way of confirming this, but it seems that the Brits always get theirs first.

Dear Son,

You are getting Apaches and so are the Brits. Everybody gets an Apache, which is a fine machine, but I'm guessing you're pretty vague when you call for support. Next time, be specific. Ask for an A-10 Thunderbolt. Some people call it the Hog. It's a hot little piece of screaming hell with a 30-mil cannon just like the Apache. It's no problem for Hogs to come in low, because they have redundant hydraulics and 900 pounds of armour shielding the pilot and the avionics. They can make it home missing a rudder, an engine, and half the wing. I know you army types love your Apache, but it only gets off 625 rounds per minute. The Hog puts out 3900 rounds per minute. That's 65 a second! And it only takes six rounds to kill a tank. How do you think Muj is going to make out in his minivan?

DEAR MA,

Where are you getting all this stuff?

DEAR SON,

Don't you remember that your father flew A-10s in the Gulf War?

DEAR MA,

Today sucked. The guys are tired of being here and so am I. When they start cutting corners and being lax in their duties I have a hard time coming down on them, given the futility of our mission here. Pranks seem to cheer them up so I kind of look the other way. They need some kind of outlet from the stress. We were patrolling a semi-rural district, nothing much going on. There was another squad ahead of us and it was turning out to be an NSF mission (no shots fired). Private Marshall decides to have a little fun, so when we come alongside Muj and his flock of sheep, Marshall drops a flash grenade and scares the living shit out of this guy. We were all having a bit of a chuckle over this when the Humvees in front stop. We were thinking maybe it was go time but no, nothing like that. The other staff sergeant got everybody out, and we're all trying to figure out what the hell this is about. Staff Sergeant Wilson wants to know who threw a flash grenade into Muj's flock of sheep. Well, I wasn't about to give up Private Marshall for a harmless prank, so we all just looked at the ground. Wilson went right off, giving my squad a lecture on the moral degradation that's been creeping into this army like a cancer. He scolded my troops, scolded me, lectured on and on about massacres in Vietnam and the breakdown of military discipline. I felt like a schoolboy sent to the principal's office, and a tiny part of me was hoping a Muj sniper would take out Wilson. It wouldn't be hard to pick out the commanding officer. He was the one shouting and waving his arms in the air and spitting into the faces of shamed soldiers. It was a long, quiet ride back to base. I couldn't even look at the men.

DEAR SON,

Please promise me you'll never let anything like that happen again. You never let someone of the same rank chew you out. You should have stood up to him face-to-face and shouted whatever. It doesn't even matter what you say. That idiot put you down because he sensed he could, just like your men play pranks because they sense they can. You're my boy and I love you, but if you expect to make it through your Mideast vacation, you're going to have to check between your legs to see if you got any. You've gotta stand up and be a man. And by the way, what is Wilson's first name?

DEAR MA,

I don't know why it would matter to you, but Wilson's first name is Peter. Our squad splattered some Muj today, so I'm less concerned about that power-tripping ass puppet. Rolling past some houses on a narrow street, we heard the tink-tink of rifle rounds hitting the hillbilly armour on our Humvee. It seemed to be coming from a tree line three hundred yards out. Kevin let off short bursts from the two-forty in the gaps between the houses, but it was hard because we were still moving. No one could confirm any kills or even see the little bastards. We pulled over behind some houses when it got a little heavier and I called for a Hog, just like you said. We had one overhead in minutes, shredding everything near the tree line, even the trees. He made another pass to let loose a Hellfire missile and on his last one we could hear the snap, crackle, pop of a cluster bomb, icing on the cake I guess. He did a flyby on his way out, twenty feet over the rooftops as all the guys were cheering, all big Hog fans now.

Dear Son,

I'm glad things are working out for you. I wish they would cover some of the success stories on the news but as usual, it's all doom and gloom. The main thing I worry about is your relationship with your men. On LiveLeak I saw a soldier tempt a child with candy in one hand, then scare him with a grenade in the other. It's not an isolated incident. I don't care about the kid. That soldier is under someone's command, and that someone is not keeping his troops in line. Wilson was way out of line scolding you like that, but he did have a point. It's a slippery slope. A soldier who naps on watch for five minutes tonight will try for ten tomorrow. You don't have to be liked, son. You should be feared and respected, like God.

DEAR MA,

Fear and respect. They've got plenty of the first one. And if they're lacking the second, I don't think I can take all the blame. They may not respect me very much but that's standard, all the way up the chain of command. Some of these guys believe in the mission. Others count the days (or hours in McMillen's case) till they can go home. No matter where they stand, no one doubts that what we're doing now isn't working. We go up and down the main streets as fast as we can, asserting ourselves as a presence but not sticking around long enough to get blown up. We don't stand our ground. We do these flyby inspections and if we aren't all killed by an IED or a kid throwing thermal grenades, we call the area "secure." The good news is that Wilson got transferred to a little hot spot known as Sadr City. Better him than me. Sometimes good things happen if you just wait it out.

DEAR SON,

I know you feel frustrated and restricted by the current arrangement, but a leader takes initiative. Do you think your lieutenant really gives a damn if you go a little bit off mission? He's got a hundred other things to worry about. When you go out on patrol you've got a start time, a finish time, and a map of the route. Throw away the map. You guys are getting hammered on major routes. I know it's easier to speed along on a nice paved surface with lights overhead, but they're waiting for you along those routes. Muj knows he's safe if he keeps to the back roads and alleys. He'll fill his shorts when he sees you sitting there in his backyard. Pull into a clearing, shut the lights off and wait. Use your night vision to check what's going on. One of those houses is going to have a lot of traffic in and out. How about kicking down the door of a house filled with bad guys? Muj can be a sneaky bastard, so why not try that for a while? I'm sending you a friend from a private-security firm. This guy isn't bound by military law and he's exempt from persecution by the Iraqi government. Can you see the possibilities? In the meantime, I've attached a diagram showing how to rig a Javelin missile to a trip wire. That will liven up the party. And remember, your job isn't being right. Your job is being effective. Congratulations soldier, you've retaken the element of surprise!

DEAR MA,

Any word from Jenny? I miss her terribly. You can tell her that I'm doing well out here. I think she would be proud. The lieutenant, even the lieutenant colonel, is very impressed with the new intel and arrests we are making, even though we are often way off our assigned route. No one seems to care about that as long as we get results. I feel like a leader and I think the men are picking up on that, but the growing pride in our unit is undermined by some asshole rotorhead in a Black Hawk who comes around to dust us every morning. First time it was funny, ha ha, good one, you got us. Yes, we have a sense of humour. But he does it every day now, and I mean every day. It's humiliating. Obviously there's nothing I can do about it, but I get the feeling the guys expect me to. How can I protect the guys from Muj if I can't protect them from one of our own?

DEAR SON,

It is the first instinct of a mother to protect her son from everything that is awful in this world. Maybe that is my problem. I never stopped doing that. If you look at it objectively, you'll realize that the question is not why bad things happen to good people. The question is why soft, unprepared, tender people survive as long as they do in this world. What I'm trying to say is that Jenny was having sex with your brother six months before you were even deployed. It's taken everything I have to keep quiet about this, because it's none of my business, but it didn't look like you were going to figure it out on your own. I hope to Christ you are better at reading oncoming traffic at a roadblock than you are at reading women. I've tried to help you, Son, but maybe that's not what you need. Maybe you need to try to walk across the desert with four litres of water. Maybe you need to run single-handed into an al Qaeda nest and shoot 'em up face-to-face. I know what I would do about your dusting problem, but I think I'll sit this one out and see what you come up with on your own.

DEAR MA,

Hearing about Jenny made me crazy mad. I have channelled all that anger into getting back at Flyboy, but you probably knew that would happen. He came in at the same time, the same approach, the same angle, with fatal predictability. Half my squad was positioned near the trucks, the other half well forward of the dusting zone. We had a dummy from the gym that we wrapped in a bedsheet for the robe, a tea towel for the head scarf. We were going to arm Dummy Muj with an AT4 but one of the guys decided an RPG would be more authentic. I don't know where he got it, but Muj looked pretty ominous with the RPG pointed skyward, sunglasses the final touch. Our secret weapon was covered with camo nets until the Black Hawk had passed over. Flyboy banked deep to dust us as usual but just as he did, we started chucking up flash grenades to scare the crap out of him, to make him think he was drawing fire, and to draw attention to Muj. You should have seen Flyboy go evasive, banking steep to get out of there, the rotors just clearing one of the tents. Ten minutes later, Flyboy comes charging up and wants to know who's in command. I stride up to him, and we're chest-to-chest, face-to-face. He says, Not funny. That was not funny. And I say, Neither is digging sand out of my shorts. He goes off when I don't apologize but I keep putting it back on him, louder, angrier, spouting anything, everything. I was like a snarling dog ready to rip his throat out and he could see it. My men could see it. I don't even know what I said, but I matched his volume until he turned away. What else could he do? Call me on a prank when he pulled one every morning? Command mystique was coming off me. Command mystique made him turn and walk away. I saw it reflected back at me by the dusted faces of my men, at that moment, in that place, winning.

DEAR SON,

You're making good progress, and now it's important to capitalize on your momentum. People will start to see you differently and you should build on that. They'll start to like you, but more importantly, they will want to be liked by you. Use this social leverage to bond your group and encourage loyalty. You'll begin to see even better results when your group starts to gel as a unit. Rotorhead had it coming, for sure, but don't forget who the real enemy is. You never know when you might need a good pilot. Maybe one day you'll be waiting for extraction and he'll decide your LZ is just a little too hot. Maybe you'll spend the night pinned down and scared shitless. It doesn't hurt to cultivate friendships where you can; otherwise, expect payback to get the better of professionalism every time.

Dear Ma,

We're getting good results in the field, and the right people are taking notice. Last night we bagged Watban Ibrahim Al-Tikriti at one of the houses we have been watching. We passed on the shock and awe and snuck into his place like a bunch of thieves, real sneaky like. The best part? The front door wasn't even locked. He is the five of spades in the Most Wanted deck and that's a big deal. Apparently Uday shot him in the leg seven times and blew his nuts off. We cornered our fierce killer with his pants down in the john and it would have been a good time to verify the rumour, but he was reading a six-month-old *Atlantic Monthly* and I got distracted by that. Seems like every single one of these Hajis wants to go out in a red-hot gun battle, so at least we deprived him of that. Since our big win, people bring me stuff. A lieutenant colonel came by to give me the old tip of the hat. My chief warrant officer just shook his hand, smiled and pretended like he knew what was going on. People want to do things for me now. Everyone wants to be part of what we've started. If there's anything we can do, they say. We're not too concerned about rank anymore; we just want to get things done. We spend a lot less time shooting at bushes and more time doing police work. It ain't soldiering but we're getting results. Everybody is coming together on this except a few Billy Bulletstops who just don't get it. I'm starting to get impatient with these see-nothing morons.

DEAR SON,

That's a good day's work, but don't get too cocky. Just when you think you know Muj, he'll change the game on you. They're called cowards in the news here because they won't stand and fight, but they're fighting the only war they can, choosing the only tactics available to an outmanned, outgunned, inferior force. To paraphrase Rummy, you've got your known unknowns and your unknown unknowns. You should be worrying about the latter here. Confidence is great around the men, but be humble in your thoughts and never stop learning about the country, the people.

DEAR MA,

The 5th just found one of our trucks loaded with money inside a gated compound. They sent for me because they thought I would know what to do. I didn't know what to do, Ma. I just sat there sweating in the back of the truck with the flap closed, staring at three pallets of shrink-wrapped American hundreds, and not a single thought came into my mind. Eugene raised the flap for a peek after ten minutes but dropped it again when I glared at him. I sat there steaming away in my gear, staring at all the bundles held down by pretty yellow cargo nets, a thick layer of dust on the plastic. They all have TBD written on them in black marker, which

Eugene thinks is short for To Be Determined. There you have it Ma, 50 million dollars, or maybe it's 500 mil, filed under "Other." It makes sense that there'd be someone looking for a pile of cash this high, but I got a feeling there's no one chasing after this. It's not missing; it's lost.

DEAR SON,

I'm sure you'll do the right thing here. I know you must be tempted, but nothing good can ever come of this. I don't know why you think no one is looking for this money. You might have a good week or a good month. Years might go by, but one day there will be a knock on the door and they will have figured it all out, all the fragments, rumours, and facts that led directly to you. There are already too many people involved. You've lost control of the information. This is not a game.

DEAR MA,

I don't think you're getting it. Iraq is a hole in the desert that we fill with money. If a little is skimmed before it gets dumped in the hole, what's the damage? Everything is under control. I worked out a schedule so that squads from the 3rd and the 5th can take turns guarding it, and every hour, the 6th detours one of their Predators to scan the neighbourhood for trouble. There has been no activity. No one is coming to pick up their lunch money. There is no intel, no notice, no bulletin, no frantic recovery mission through normal lines of communication or back channels. No one cares. I know what you mean about losing control though. It's been two days and already we have leakage. The nearest pallet load has been cut open and is missing about a cubic foot of cash.

DEAR SON,

Some things can be overlooked, and some things will never be forgiven. Do you want to find out the hard way how this will turn out? It's not too late to salvage this situation. Just say you delayed in reporting the money because you were using it as bait to catch some Muj. You'll get into trouble for not reporting it earlier, but the fallout will be relatively minor.

DEAR MA,

Let's be clear: I'm not stealing. This is redirected operational money. We're running a smarter war now. No one is better at killing Muj than another Muj. Our translator hooked us up with Fareed, a local who's plugged in to everything, including the twenty-odd groups fighting for power here, our troop rotations, patrol routes, and a whole lot of other stuff he shouldn't know. Now that we're buying local, we've been turning this town upside down. We are branching out, letting some of Fareed's friends handle our problems directly. Why endanger ourselves when we can hire local mercs? Leakage continues, but I can't really hold it against the guys. The war machine makes more money than God here, and even the snake eaters make a grand a day. Why should we expect these clueless meat shields to take it in the nuts for nothing? They deserve a little bonus for good performance. Our operations are so effective they're five to a cell in the Al Baatra Prison.

DEAR SON,

There's comes a point when even Mama can't help. If you continue down this road, you'll be on your own. There are people there who care about you, about your future. How much cash are we talking about?

DEAR MA,

I don't know. The pallets are square and come up to my waist. Each bunch of hundreds is about an inch thick. You figure it out. My sources tell me some idiot just paid his buddy a grand to get him a cheeseburger from the mess hall. WTF. Monkeys, I tell ya, all of them. Monkeys. It really does make you think differently about your pay with these Baghdad Bucks floating around. Money doesn't mean what it used to. There are even some bills starting to show up on Iraqi locals. I suppose I should have told these monkeys to shut their dick traps, but now everyone wants to visit the money truck. Was I wrong to expect more of them, Ma?

DEAR SON,

Do all the rigid rules, traditions, and protocols start to make sense now? We need them to maintain order. Power isn't the same as authority, Son.

DEAR MA,

Friday night was race night. I sat in my chair with a six-pack and looked up at the stars while Painface played on my iPod. It was Predator vs. Alien and everybody was pretty excited as the drones did their laps around the markers, everyone looking down at the pilot's laptop and then up at the sky. There were friendly bets with cigarettes and beer, until one of my flunky idiots pulled out a bundle of Baghdad Bucks. The hush was only temporary and soon the bills were flying. I work with monkeys, Ma. No discretion. I don't know why I thought the guys would be smarter than that. This queasy feeling, I would assume, is caused by having my fate controlled by morons. I didn't stop it, because gambling is important here. It lets them win at something. Everybody is screaming as Team Alien takes the final lap. The winner has to fly under the finish line, a wire seven metres off the deck we've strung between two poles. Team Alien is blocking the approach, so Team Predator tries to get underneath him and plows their drone into a tree. $5,000,000. I hear the guys have started to weigh money instead of counting it, like it was cocaine or something. I reckon the drone is about 10 kilos of Baghdad Bucks. Some thought repair might be an option, but when we got to the site it looked like a bag of smashed assholes. Then a fight broke out, one beefy MP doing serious damage with his Semper Fu.

DEAR SON,

Remember when you were seven and I forbade you from riding your bike on the street, but you did it anyway? Remember how I came out and starting screaming at you for pedaling out into traffic when I told you to stay in our yard? I took your bike away and told you I was going to sell it. Later, after I had calmed down and was sure you understood the dangers of riding on the road, I forgave you for your defiance and let you ride again. Do you remember that? The forgiveness and compassion I showed you? You don't get any of that in a military prison.

DEAR MA,

These Muj, Ma, they kill me. One of Fareed's tips led us to a crappy hovel in the southeast corner of sector 8. We set up, front and back, and waited. They're getting better with booby traps, so I don't like entering places much anymore. No need for it really. Ali Baba comes flying out at us with his knife held high, screaming Allahu Akbar this and la-la-la-la that, yammering on how they do about God being great and let's go hole another American. I look behind him, around him, not fooled by his diversion. To come at us like that he would have set up snipers on the roof, his backup in the shadows of a dark doorway on our flank. I was ready to fire my 40 mike-mike into every open hole, but there was only this one guy taking on our whole squad with his knife, like the boys in the last scene in *Butch Cassidy and the Sundance Kid*, surrounded, outnumbered, doomed. I figured one shot to the chest would do it, but no, he didn't even flinch, so everybody opened up on him, until someone's lucky bullet bit into something vital and he crumpled to the ground. He had that look that I've seen so many times before, as he lay there sucking his last sharp breaths, relieved to die like that, to bleed out into the sand. Now there's a guy who believes in Heaven. I just don't know what to do with these fuckheads. They're fearless, they keep coming, and there's an endless supply. Even if we could press a button and magically vaporize all the Muj in Iraq, there's another batch of fourteen-year-olds being trained in northern Pakistan. Shooting them down is like shooting at flies in a pig barn.

Dear Son,

Your father used to talk about VC being like mosquitos. They were small and easily squashed but they came on in clouds and bled you dry, one small bite at a time. We will win this with superior firepower and technology. There are 15,000 predators in use. I guess 14,999 now, thanks to the boys! It won't be long before you'll be able to fly your drone over Iraq from the comfort of an apartment in West Virginia. Stay the course. The tide will turn.

Dear Ma,

The tide may turn, but we're in a desert. Last night, friends of ours wanted to show us what a good job they were doing. Fareed's associates were eager to show their appreciation for all the Baghdad Bucks that were flowing into their circle. We entered the ground floor of a house, where they had a bad guy bound and gagged on the floor. He looked pretty out of it, like he had been drugged. I like a show as much as the next guy, Ma, but I barely had time to sit in the seat of honour before they whipped out a knife and carved off his left hand. Then his right hand and both feet. He was wriggling a little but not much, considering, and the way they had tied cord tightly at the joints there was hardly any blood. They didn't want him to bleed out, of course, because the whole point was that he would live without hands and feet. That's better than a simple execution. I didn't even have time to think, completely ambushed by these savages, and I smiled the smile of anyone receiving a gift from an important person. I'm pretty sure Eugene threw up a little bit but then swallowed it, recovering nicely, realizing what was at stake. All I could think was how sharp a knife would have to be to cut through joints like they were nothing.

DEAR SON,

That's not you. That's nothing to do with you. I'm sure they didn't even tell you what your digitless friend did. How do you know Fareed isn't part of a hard-core faction that is settling old scores and getting paid by you to do it? That's what I would do if I were in his position. Are you finding bomb gear and RPGs in those houses you're tossing, or is it just the odd AK in the closet? That's the equivalent of a 9-mil in the night-table drawer in America. You have no way of verifying who's AQ and who's not, do you? What happened to playing detective? You were doing so well on your own, and now it sounds like you are totally dependent on Fareed.

DEAR MA,

Last email for a while. Things are getting a little complicated here. Undoing is a little harder than doing, you know? I spent most of the day waiting for the right wind, as you probably know by now. Conditions were calm until later in the afternoon, and when we caught the breeze, I ordered the money truck to its new location on the outskirts of the city. The EOD guys strapped some charges to the chassis, and we backed off 500 metres, behind a rocky outcrop. Then your crusty old friend found me, standing above me where I lay on the ground, his fat head blocking out the sun. He was hilarious, standing there in full military dress, his chest full of medals sparkling in the sun. Where did you dig up that old coot?

He said, looks like you got yourself a real bag of dicks there, son, but we can fix this. It was impossible to ignore his words, low and rumbling like a freight train. He had command mystique, giving low, smooth orders that simply had to be obeyed. I turned to my EOD guy and said, Blow the truck, and instead of following my orders, he looked up at the silver hair for approval. I said, Blow the truck, Specialist Murphy. It rained money on Baghdad for twenty minutes. I can't confirm or deny, I have no knowledge but mostly, Ma, I don't remember.

I SEE A MAN

FOR A WEEK THERE'S DRIZZLE WITH A
chance of drizzle from the Vancouver sky, but today it's sunny and
cold, with frost where the sun can't reach. My car idles in the air-
port parkade with my fingers still on the ignition. House calls
change the relationship. I shouldn't have come, but Paul is desperate to resolve conflicts with his father that have festered since
childhood. He's fifty-four.

Sometimes I suggest reading material to clients. Sometimes I
wish I had a book with a spring-loaded boxing glove that would
pop out and punch Paul in the head. I have this un-counsellor-like
wish more often than I'd like. When I think of this in the middle
of a session, my diaphragm starts spasming with laughter and I
have to cough to cover it. I wonder if I have more unprofessional
thoughts than the average counsellor. Here's another unprofessional thought: I really want to meet Paul's father, and not only
to resolve Paul's issues. Sedrick Prudhomme has his own Wikipe-
dia entry and hundreds of other articles and interviews about the
rise of his Bezaruti fashion line. Paul is waiting on a bench in the
US Departures area, splitting his attention between CNN and a

crumpled list of talking points. We sit and wait for the great man.

Ninety minutes later, a woman in her thirties marches toward us and abruptly stops. She asks if he is Paul Prudhomme, although she seems to have no doubt. She may not be perfect but I can't see any flaws, from the photo-shoot-ready black hair to the crisp navy-blue suit that hugs her shape, the skirt tapering down to naturally tanned legs. We follow her to the limo, her diamond-hard calves popping out with each step. In the limo my search becomes more desperate, scanning her face now for a tiny glob of mascara, some sand in her eye, a crooked tooth. Her scuff-free shoes look like they've never touched the ground, the heel height somewhere between call girl and accountant, the stitching precise and measured, not hastily yanked through a sewing machine by a Chinese wage slave.

—Can I help you with something?

I look up from her shoe.

—Are those Jimmy Choo?

—No.

Apparently there are rules we should follow when we meet with Sedrick at the South Terminal, where the private jets land. The meeting will end at exactly 1600h. The following topics are off-limits: money, loans, gifts, business opportunities and charity. We should know we are quite fortunate that Mr. Prudhomme has granted a full hour of exclusive one-on-one access.

—You know he's my father, right?

—I know that and many other things about you.

We get a tight, sharp smile before she continues with the

briefing. Under no circumstances are we to interrupt Mr. Prud-homme while he is talking. If we have something to say, we should raise our hands. During our meeting, Mr. Prudhomme may be called away for a variety of reasons. This is unavoidable. We don't get to the jet until 3:15 p.m., the hangars casting long shadows in the weak November light. It is impossible to ignore the symbolic power of getting out of a limo and into a private jet, even if it's someone else's and we won't be leaving the ground. Sedrick once told Paul that a measure of status among the rich was having a jet with headroom. How much do we grow past our childlike selves? As much as the world demands of us. A top-heavy monster in a suit intercepts us before we can step up the ladder. He pats us down and makes us take off our shoes while an old man watches from the window. Sedrick plays host as we step on board, shaking his son's hand.

—Can I get you something?

—Yeah, I'll have my dignity back, and a gin and tonic.

We are finally introduced to our escort, Simone, and it looks like she'll be staying with us for the meeting. Sedrick says Simone is with him everywhere, always. As what, I wonder. Memory? Conscience? Massage therapist? Courtesan? All of the above? How many years before she's replaced by a newer model a decade away from crow's-feet?

Sedrick has slicked-back hair like some greasy spit-combing preacher from the South. The suit is probably his own design, very nice with a black shirt and no tie. I'm drawn to the shoes but pass on closer inspection. It's unfair to judge him instantly, but it looks like nothing good has ever come from that mouth. The hardened embouchure of his lips has issued battle cries, it has punished, insisted, threatened, chastised and fired. It's hard to imagine those lips gently kissing a baby's cheek, that mouth whispering something kind to a lover. He did not shake my hand, offer me a drink, or even look at me. That's how he controls. If Sedrick does not look at me or talk to me, I don't exist.

Paul starts to lay it all out and I want to touch his arm and tell him to stop, retreat, it's a trap. I made the following assumptions about Sedrick: fashion, artistic, sensitive, open. The reality of Sedrick is fashion, artistic, sadistic, closed. Nothing will stop Paul as he reviews injuries of the past: The house was always full of busy people, and he learned early on that everyone else's needs were more important than his own. If they were short a chair for dinner, he would give up his and sit on the kitchen bench. If there were overnight guests from Munich, he would give up his bed and sleep on the couch. Soccer game or fashion show, the winner was always clear.

Sedrick made a great show of democracy, running family meetings where each one had a say, but somehow the votes were never counted. What Paul wanted was not important. The early lessons of childhood are still remembered as he drives along the highway, often checking the mirror to see if he's slowing someone down, ready to pull to the side, or in the grocery store, always making sure he doesn't block someone else's path with his cart.

—Are you planning to sue me for some kind of childhood abuse? Is that your angle? How much to make you go away?

Sedrick has opened his chequebook and has his pen ready. Paul looks defeated and goes silent, so I attempt a summary of what we're working on. Those early lessons have carried through to Paul's adult life, affecting the relationships in his family, his work, and the larger world. Since Paul's issues started with childhood, Sedrick's memory or perspective on that period might help us clarify or correct some of our working assumptions.

—The case you make is very weak, totally without merit, but since I am in a rush, I'm willing to pay Paul to never again use the following words in my presence: relationship, childhood and issue. I should also mention that it's not my fault that Paul has done nothing with his life. No wife, no kids, and he works in a toy factory.

—It is not a toy factory. I make violins. I am a luthier.

—Use whatever fancy name you like. It's still making toys. I didn't raise you to be this.

—What makes you think you raised me at all?

Paul tries to justify his existence in a way that will never please his father. Ranta Kosilla of the Cleveland Philharmonic recently ordered two of his violins, but Paul will never win the fight for his father's approval, because his father knows how much power can be gained by withholding it. Simone does her best to give us privacy, a bit of a trick sitting three feet away but she tries, staring out the window at other planes taking off. Perhaps she is uncomfortable seeing a fifty-four-year-old man cry.

The story of Paul's ex-fiancée comes out as it always does, and Sedrick rolls his eyes. I wonder if he has heard it as many times as I have. Sedrick never approved of the woman Paul proposed to when he was thirty-five. He was certain she was an untrustworthy gold-digger and to prove it, he slept with her on his yacht a week before the marriage. He considered it a favour he had done for his son, saving him years of grief. I mean, what kind of woman would sleep with her fiancé's father? One that was after the money. And she did go on to prove herself by marrying a seventy-two-year-old billionaire shipping magnate.

Sedrick's hand still holds the pen above the cheque. Simone is editing addresses in her phone. I start thinking about Kevin Kline, waiting for me at the door with his tail waving slowly back and forth like a question mark, able to tell from the quality of the light that I'm late. I can't even imagine a positive direction our meeting might take. We should go. Light is failing. Who knows what Sedrick turns into after dark?

—I don't want your money. I want you to admit that you hurt me.

Oh, god. I've heard it before, but in the presence of Sedrick it just sounds pathetic. Paul doesn't seem to know his father at all. Money has a way of making people right. It doesn't matter what you did; if you end up rich, you must have been right. You dictate a self-flattering, convenient reality and impose it on those around you. No one argues with a billion dollars. Paul renounces the money. He says he doesn't want it. Sedrick nods his head and believes none of it, the pen still poised.

—No one ever says no to the money. That isn't a theory or a guess. In forty years of experience, no one has ever said no to the money. You've come to me crying with brave words and all kinds of demands, but you'll leave with a cheque tucked in your pocket. You think you're going to be the exception to the rule? Do you think you're exceptional? Now why don't you take the cheque and your fag therapist and get on your way?

—He's not gay.

—Wake up! Did you see the way he was sitting? Look at the clothes he's wearing. Look at the back of his neck. What kind of car does he drive?

Paul looks at me with a panicked look.

—I drive a Miata.

—You see? Even his car is gay! If you're taking advice from this half-a-man, it's not surprising you're so fucked up. I've got a whole squad of gays working for me, but I would never let one into my head. You want to fix your head, go up to the cabin and chop some wood.

We're done here. This disaster has set my client back months. Forget about wrapping up, or sanding off rough edges. We just have to get the fuck off this plane before it gets worse. Sedrick is busy writing a cheque when the engines start winding up at 4:00 p.m. to the second. Paul stands to leave, taking the cheque as he passes his father, but I pause in front of him, fighting the urge to curse him out. He doesn't like me but he saw me, noticed the way I sat, my grooming, my clothes. I exist.

—You don't get a cheque.

—You don't get my respect.

—You'd respect me if you got a cheque.

As soon as I step off, the ladder is hauled up to the closed position and the jet starts moving. Paul wants to know why I lied to him. Announcing my orientation is not part of my relationship with a client. I wonder what difference it makes. I'm a professional listener. How would that be affected by whom and how I love? What has changed in the last hour? I was keen to meet someone who turned out to be a jerk. Paul had false assumptions about his counsellor. The only one proceeding through his day with some certainty, all assumptions and predictions intact, is Sedrick Prud-homme, jetting to elevations far beyond the common man.

The sixteen-year-old me worked hard to get a night at home with my father. He never seemed to do much except watch TV, but when I asked for some time for the two of us he seemed anxious, as if he were sacrificing half a dozen more exciting options. Mother had agreed to go to her weekly bridge night and stay a little longer than usual. I didn't even have to say the words to her the night before. She had known since I was eight. I left my body and watched me and my father sit in the kitchen with our hands on the table, each word out of my mouth one word closer to the three words I needed to say: I am gay. You could pile up hundreds or thousands of words in front of those three and it would not weaken their devastating force. The bomb dropped. The mushroom cloud flashed its brilliant beauty. The shock wave knocked down everything. All that was left was fallout.

Dad slouched, looking at a spot in the centre of the table. He got up, pulled a suitcase down from the back-closet shelf, and started stuffing some of my clothes into it. He put it on the front steps and went to his office. A few minutes later, he came back to where I stood in the hallway. He wouldn't look at me as he held out a cheque in one hand and pointed to the door with the other as if I were a badly behaved dog. I took his cheque but didn't look at it. I didn't want to see how much it was worth to him to get rid of me. I walked to the door, turned around, ripped his cheque into tiny pieces and blew them off my palm. Traumatic yes, but also an invigorating renewal.

Paul sits as close to his door as he can. He ignores me when I ask him if he needs a ride somewhere and I have no empathy, sympathy, or interest in him right now. The angel of healing and reconciliation has been shot dead, or maybe sucked into the intake of a jet engine. Do I owe it to the world, to my profession, to continue treating my homophobic client? More crying and a continuing refusal to look at me. Paul gets out when we reach the main terminal. I stay in the back, waiting to see what the driver will do. He looks Chilean, short, slightly overweight. He is texting someone on his cell phone while he waits for me to leave. I get out, open the front door, and get back in.

—Look at me. Do you see me? What do you see?

—I see a man.

I reach out to touch his cheek and he moves his head away. I stop my hand but don't put it down. Some of the stiffness seems to leave his body, and I touch his jawbone. The Chilean has looked at me. He is no longer a part of the car's driving mechanism, and I am no longer cargo. He sees me. He sees a man.

KILLERS ARE USEFUL

AN IDIOT STAGGERS INTO CAMP IN THE middle of the afternoon. I tell him to stop but he keeps coming, reaching for me with a crazed grin. After I knee him in the groin, I realize he was trying to shake my hand. A gentleman. I'm alone and Kayla has the gun but it seems this one, curled up like a baby on the ground, is not a threat. A search of his briefcase confirms that he is, in fact, an idiot. He has a ziplock bag of money, a box of memory sticks, a cell phone, and some clothes. Most people this dumb are already dead. Sometimes a group will send a scout into our camp to count people, food, weapons, but I have the feeling this one's a lone straggler from the city. If he came straight down the Lougheed Highway he's very lucky. If he went overland, through the bush, over barbed wire, across the Pitt River, then it's been a tough slog and he deserves credit. He stops moaning long enough to speak.

—I mean you no harm.

Definitely the funniest thing I've heard all month, idiot crawling in the dirt, assuring me he's not a threat.

—May I have some food?

—No.

—Please. I'm very hungry.

—How about this? You sit there and shut up and I won't cave your head in.

I wonder whether bitchiness and aggression are signs of early pregnancy. My period is late, very late, but how late is late enough to announce that there might be another joining our group? Kayla comes out of the bush with Rob and Eric. Amin and Ben are still upstream testing a fishnet made of wool. Kayla makes the intruder spread-eagle and searches him, something I forgot to do. No surprises, anyway. There used to be more demanding fools like this one, desperate to tell their stories, thinking we would care. You will never hear one of these leeches offer to show you how to handload 12-gauge shells, or remove plaque from teeth, or butcher a pig, or smoke fish. No. They all want something for nothing. Eric takes the shotgun from Kayla and rests it against the intruder's forehead.

—Please don't kill me.

—Shut the fuck up and listen to what I have to tell you. My name is Eric.

—My name is—

—You don't have a name until you do something useful. You can share one meal with us if you go down to that farmhouse and find something we need.

—What do you need?

—Think. You obviously didn't do much of that before you left home, so this is your second chance. Think very hard about what might be useful and bring it back to us.

No-Name starts stuffing his things into his bag, but Eric waves the end of the barrel in his face.

—Leave it.

No-Name will get his stuff back, but he doesn't know that. Eric seems to enjoy this, some stranger twisted by anger and fear, powerless to negotiate or reason with the guy who has a gun pointed at his head. No-Name is a worm, potentially trouble, definitely a pain, but I feel for him as he backs away from our group, leaving behind his most important things, things he thought would help him survive, things that gave him the feeling he had some control over his world. From the back he looks like a well-dressed version of my ex-husband. The suit jacket looks tailor-made, and the shoes! Italian slip-ons with tassels! Hunched over and beaten, the pathetic idiot leaves our camp on his way to the farmhouse. I grab the shotgun from Eric and catch up to him, suddenly protective of such an easy mark. Eric shouts after me.

—Don't help him. He's got to find something on his own.

No-Name seems frightened at first, less so when I crack open the breech of the gun and hang it over my forearm. Away from camp, I start talking and can't stop, energized by this new person, someone whose personal tics I have not catalogued, who can tell me something new about himself or the world. In the city, people dropped garbage out of their windows, and then the rats came. He tried to persuade them to dump their garbage in the bay where it would be taken out to sea, but he couldn't even get them to dig holes for their own shit. There is an attractive man in there, underneath the beard, the dirt, the BO. Maybe he'll be able to charm

Old Lady Templeton, but we'll probably have to do some kind of chore, heavy lifting that's too much for the old man, or something in the barn. Those expensive shoes will be covered in pig shit by the end of this.

His name is Anthony, never Tony. I'm sure he was once respected in his world, but out here we'll call him Tony if we want to. We'll call him Mary, or Scumbag, or Leech, or Donor if we want to. He'll learn. We find a Ford Windstar on the side of the road where it ran out of gas. It hasn't been here long, but there's nothing I can use except a Coffee Crisp I find wedged into the backseat. I split it with Tony on the condition that he doesn't tell the others. When we get to the farm I leave the shotgun on the steps, knock on the door, and step back thirty feet. I wait a couple of minutes and then try again. The door is unlocked but the stench knocks me back.

—Something is rotting in there, Anthony. I hope you have a strong stomach.

He does not. He's bug-eyed and sputtering when he comes out: corpses, eaten, flies, blood. Tony doesn't seem to realize we're well past the point of calling someone else to do something we'd rather not do. I wait for him to get over it. He's drooling with his head between his legs, just short of puking.

—You heard what Eric said, right? You have to get something useful or you're not eating with us tonight.

Brave Tony puts his hand back on the doorknob and that's as far as he gets. I send him out to search the barn. My turn to visit the Templetons. They're both at the kitchen table. He's facedown in a plate of potatoes with a bullet in the back of his head and she's on the floor, curled around the legs of a chair, footprints in her blood leading to the door. The rat that comes out of her mouth looks a little territorial. The kitchen has been stripped, but the last guests may have left something upstairs. In her closet, the wardrobe is intact, but how much of the smell will her clothes absorb and for how long? Will there ever be a time when I'm desperate enough to wear the clothes she wore? I can see Tony from the bedroom window as he stands, looking lost, near the barn. There is nothing left. All the bedding has been taken, all the sheets and towels. I could rip off some wood from the barn but there is no shortage of wood in the bush. Back in the kitchen I'm annoyed at the waste of it, the selfishness of those assholes who left the Templetons here to rot instead of dragging them outside. Somebody could have lived here, but not now, not with a colony of rats, their small black turds everywhere, the stench of rotting guts working its way into the wood. They could have used the old geezers to fatten a pig or something but no, a bullet in the head and good-bye.

I take the toaster. The shiny metal covering can be cut into fishing lures, the cord split in two and used as rope, the tiny, thin wires of the heating elements used for . . . I don't know, but I'll think of something by the time I get back to camp. Eric isn't going to be impressed but maybe this will be enough to get Tony fed. Why I would care I don't know. Tony meets me at the door with a big smile. The great provider has a shirt pouch full of muddy, beautiful potatoes and carrots. The main garden behind the house was torn apart months ago but there's a tiny hidden plot that sits in a fallow field, far from any road, path, or building.

Tony is okay. We celebrate back at camp, everyone taking turns smelling a carrot, patting Tony on the back. Tonight the fire is bigger than usual and Ben comes back from the cache with two cans each of tuna and beans. Together with the vegetables, they make a feast. In the morning, Eric offers to help Tony pack his things, a much gentler eviction than usual. Tony has forgotten the exact terms of his stay here and seems to think he can convince us that he is useful enough to stay.

—There are more potatoes and carrots. I can show you where.

—We already know where they are. You showed Tanya, remember?

—I have money. I have $900,000 on this disk.

—You might as well have 900,000 buttons. No, I take that back. Buttons would be useful. You don't know what anything is worth. A laying chicken is worth a piglet. A jar of vitamins is worth some antibiotics. A rifle is worth a plow. A fishing lure is worth a tube of fire starter.

—I can tie knots.

That's enough to make Eric shut up for a second. I say we'd use less rope on the tarps if we knew how to tie proper knots. It would help with traps and fishing, too. Eric seems annoyed by my defense of the leech, and there's something else in his look, too: ownership. He crawled under my covers while the others were searching for the headwaters of the stream and he restarted feelings I thought were dead forever. But then he came inside me. Of course he did. Every morning after, I prayed for my period. Eric is shaking his head, turning the others against Tony. Knot tying would be good, but it could be taught in an afternoon and the group would need something of lasting value.

—I have a boat.

Tony's fifty-foot sailboat might have been pillaged for stores by now but most likely the important gear is untouched. There are easier boats at the False Creek Marina and much richer targets on shore. The boat has three double cabins and room for more in the central cabin. It makes an excellent fishing platform and comes stocked with two complete sets of dive gear and traps for crabs and prawns. More importantly, it's big enough to make an ocean crossing, to Hawaii for example, which is where the prevailing winds would take us. It's the perfect climate for outdoor living, no more cold and wet for eight months a year. Eric and Ben take turns finding holes in the plan, countering with reservations, problems, doubts, but I'm already on the beach with a warm wind blowing off the ocean as the baby nurses, soon old enough to eat finger bananas and chunks of sweet, warm pineapple as we fall asleep in a hammock to the sound of swishing palm leaves.

—I will go with you.

Everyone looks at me, then Eric, to see what he'll do.

—If you leave here, you leave with nothing.

It would be more accurate to say that they have nothing if I leave. I do most of the cooking, including the drying of meat and long-term storage of vegetables. I scavenged our bedding during the November riots when the truck still had gas. I'm the one who picked up Ben and Kayla by the side of the road as they waited to be stripped of everything by the next person with a gun. I follow Tony to the stream, where he is on his hands and knees drinking from the toilet section, unaware that clean water is thirty feet upstream. I tap on his shoulder as he slurps away like a dog.

—I want to go with you on your boat.

—I don't think Eric would like that.

—We're not ... He's not ... He doesn't own me.

—He's not the alpha dog?

Eric would love to be called the alpha dog. He has emerged as a sort of leader where none is required, issuing orders when everyone knows what to do. How did it happen? How did our co-op slide into dictatorship? I watch water drip off Tony's beard. Eric is just a man. Tony is a father. He smiles at me for the second time just as Eric cracks him in the head with a tree branch, diving on top of his back to keep Tony's head under water. I pick up the branch and start beating Eric but it's like breaking wood over a boulder. Soon I'm exhausted and the Italian loafers with tassels are no longer thrashing against the bank.

—He was going to take me to Hawaii.

—I don't want you to go to Hawaii.

Eric pulls off Tony's jacket, belt, shoes, and sends the rest, the useless parts, downstream. When he hangs up the jacket to dry back at the camp, the debate about Tony ends. Eric mentions the shoes are Euro size forty-four if anyone is interested.

That night, I stand over Eric just inside the entrance of his tent. The murderer has no problem sleeping. Would a baby be safe around a ruthless pragmatist? Would a baby be safe around anyone

other than a ruthless pragmatist? I would ask Tony, but he's floating down to the ocean while the seagulls pluck out his eyeballs and
pick at his wound. When he sinks, the crabs will take over. I wave
the barrel of the shotgun in Eric's direction, but he doesn't lunge
at me like a coiled snake. He doesn't overpower me. He's sleeping.
Like a baby.

LAKE PINOT

HANNAH'S ARM EXTENDS TOWARD US like she's a curler who has just released a rock, long after she has pushed the stern of our canoe over grinding rocks and onto a massive liquid mirror. On the shoreline, Christians wave, whistle and shout standard encouragement to the little voyageurs in my care. Water drips off the tip of my paddle, each drop sending out rings of tiny waves on the glass-calm water.

I've canoed before. I had hoped this modest claim would imply a minimal level of experience, but all Hannah heard was that I was an expert, and she told this to anyone who would listen. Now I'm leading an expedition with three twelve-year-olds I don't know, whose parents I don't know, into territory I don't know, so I can teach them nautical skills, survival skills, camping skills, all within the context of good Christian fellowship. Our mission is to paddle from Camp Kahanisota across Kowpers Lake, the deepest in British Columbia, to a vaguely defined distant shore. When I glance back and see her waving and laughing with her friends, it seems slightly less absurd that I would do this. There's no point in getting mad about it. That's just what my luscious Christian does.

She takes a few short words and runs with them.

The last time I was in a canoe, we capsized and got mild hypothermia. That's a lesson I won't be sharing with the boys. Instead they will learn about the centre of gravity and what it can do for you, or to you. Wind blow, stay low. Switching sides all the time can be avoided if the stern paddler sometimes drags his paddle like a rudder. The J-stroke lets you paddle and steer. Luke, my forward paddler, is taking it all in, making adjustments to his form as I speak. Levi isn't interested. His buddy Mark copies this aloofness, along with Levi's speech, gestures, vocabulary and sarcasm. Sixty-six percent of my paddling class is not paying attention, drawn instead to a massive eagle's nest, which generates some excitement, but not much and not for long.

Levi brings us to that moment in every canoe trip when some kid discovers that if you swing your paddle forward and let the tip bite into the lake, you can launch an arc of water at least twenty feet. Luke and I paddle out of range, closer to huge sections of forest in Christmas colours, red needles of trees killed by pine beetles set against remaining green ones. No one saw that coming. Staying with the catastrophe theme, I start itemizing a list of things that could go wrong out here and it scares the hell out of me. Camp Kahanisota is impossible to separate from the rest of the shoreline now. Our cheering fans will have forgotten us.

You know when you're walking past a gym in Kitsilano and in the few seconds it takes to pass the floor-to-ceiling window you see a woman doing bench presses, and she glances at you but not in a way that suggests she thinks of you as an insect or a predator or dog dirt but in an open way, free of any big-city sensibility, a way that suggests she is in Kitsilano but not of it, and you go into the gym and ask if there is a trial membership or a day pass and you buy outrageously overpriced gym wear so you can be around her and eventually talk to her? Before I knew her name I wanted to be with the woman who tried to hide her body in baggy grey sweats when she worked out. If some people give off light and others absorb it, she is the sun.

Levi takes off his life vest and I tell him to put it back on. If he doesn't obey me in the next thirty seconds, I'm sunk for the rest of the trip. I tell him again, and more power slips away. First he pretends not to hear and then, without looking at me directly, he claims it's too hot to wear a vest. Mark looks at Levi, then at me, and takes his off too, now that Levi has proven I'm harmless. The two of them start pulling hard to be the first ones on land. Luke and I are still a hundred feet from shore when the others run off into the woods. I yell for them to stop, and once again, weakly. If they were here I could ask them, Have you ever thought about how it would feel to have your neck ripped out by a cougar? Yes you, the tender morsel, a light load easily dragged. And bears can smell blood from forty miles away. Luke looks at me differently too, now that I've been broken, perhaps waiting for me to grasp real power like other adults do.

—What are we going to do now?

—Are you one of those kids who asks that every fifteen minutes?

—No.

—So you can entertain yourself?

—I excel at self-entertainment.

—Okay, you can do whatever you want as long as you stay close to the campsite. I'm just going to sit here for a while.

I slump against a tree and study whatever I can take in without moving my head. There is reasonable protection from the wind here, trees fairly close to the bank, plenty of flat spots without tree roots for the tents. The bugs aren't bad, but we'll have to wait until dusk for the real test. No predator droppings in the vicinity. Enough wood within reach to make a decent fire. If we had to walk out along a land route we'd be hooped: no pathways or roads that I can see. We've barely started and I know I'm not going to make it. Isolating myself with a bunch of kids? Was that my idea or the devil's? My heart is racing and I've lost ten pounds just from sweating, which will get worse now that we're on land again. If those brat kids come back alive, I'm going to beat them to death. Luke, God bless him, does a great job of staying out of my face, studying the bore patterns of the pine beetle and flipping over rocks by the shore to collect samples. I'm not kidding. He has sample jars.

While the other boys are gone, we begin to unload the canoes and I think of ways to explain the death of my two young rebels. Your son ran off in the woods and I didn't chase after him because I didn't like him. I hear they found his remains in some bear scat. His watch was intact. Would you like me to get it for you? The tent is a three-dimensional exam in physics and geometry. I let Luke in on it, pretending to provide him an opportunity to sharpen his problem-solving skills, although it seems obvious in seconds that nothing on Luke needs sharpening.

—The poles go through those fabric sleeves.

Of course they do. Any fool could see that. Both canoes are emptied and turned over, our supplies are stacked and ready for inspection, the tents are up, the foams are out, and the sleeping bags are open. No food. I rifle through everything one more time. No food.

On the other side of the lake there's a woman. Everyone likes her and wants to be near her. Within minutes of my first sighting, I was on the bench next to hers, trying to guess what a decent weight might be on the bench press for a man. She turned, smiled, and asked me to spot her. Somewhere between the sixth and seventh rep, obsession set in.

—Don't help so much. You're doing them for me.

It seemed fair to ask her to spot me as I put on twice the weight she was benching. It was too much and my arms started shaking, forcing her to move forward to get under the weight, her crotch only inches from my face. The bar crashed back into the cradle and I couldn't look at her until she punched my shoulder, teasing me for being such a wimp. She wasn't mad, or creeped out by the sleazy thing that just happened. It didn't even occur to her. She said, Gym shorts look great with dress shoes, and then she winked. Coffee? I asked. Yes, she said.

I stare at the package of marshmallows Hannah snuck into my bag. I imagine feeding them to a solemn line of starving boys, hands out for their ration. Hannah put spongy treats in my pack, but she also took something out. From Luke's expression I can tell

I'm not hiding it well.

—Are you okay, Alan?

—I'm fine.

There has never been a bigger lie. Salvation is miles away at the far end of the lake, sitting in her bag, or the truck, or maybe the garbage. She doesn't know what the canteen means to me, or worse, she does. Rebels for Christ return, stomping loudly through the bush.

—We saw a bear.

—Good, that's one thing we don't have to worry about. They won't be attracted to our food, because we don't have any.

You'd think I had told them their families were dead. Mark starts to cry and Levi whines until I snap.

—Do you want me to call your mom and get her to bring you a peanut butter sandwich?

—That would be better than this.

—Okay guys, listen up. I've got a secret to share. You're not going to die if you miss a couple of meals. Now shut up about it already. You can live for three weeks without food.

—No water either?

—There's about a billion litres right in front of you, Levi. Help yourself.

—This is bullshit. We're going back.

—No, you're not. It'll be dark soon.

—Yes, I am. Come on, Mark.

I look at Luke and smile. The Rebel Christians turn their canoe over and drag it down to the water. Mark gets in and Levi pushes off, dragging himself in over the stern.

—Hey, where are the paddles?!

There's no response from us as they drift, a light breeze eventually bringing them back to shore downwind from our camp. Our prank is forgotten when Luke finds fishhooks and line in our gear, automatic competition setting in as we hunt for sticks and improvise lures with tinfoil, hoping for fried fish with a side of marshmallows. The Rebel Christians get bored first, the tempo of fishing unable to match the Xbox. My toes get wrinkly as I stand in two feet of water, willing Luke to quit. I can't teach him a lesson in perseverance until he does. Ideally, Luke gives up and then a minute later I catch a fish—that's supposed to be the lesson. Failing that, I can teach a different lesson, one about cutting your losses, recognizing when you've made a mistake, how to know when perseverance has crossed the line over to stupidity, and other valid reasons to give up. Luke hangs on for two hours after I wade to shore, without frustration, without fatigue, a scientist isolating variables: a little foil, no foil, a lot of foil, movement, no movement, deep, shallow, worm, no worm, prayer, no prayer. Twenty minutes after sunset he wades to shore and mentions quietly that the probabilities were never very good.

—Levi, I don't suppose you've got something to drink tucked away in that bag of yours.

—There's about a billion litres right in front of you, Al.

—You know what I mean. A drink drink. Because if you did, you wouldn't get in trouble if you told me about it. I wouldn't tell anybody.

—Sorry, Alan, I don't know what you mean.

—I'll give you a hundred bucks if you have anything in your bag. That's what I mean.

And it hasn't even started.

Everything I asked from Hannah I received. She agreed to go for coffee after our workout. She allowed me to walk her home. She didn't resist when I leaned forward to kiss her, and she didn't attempt to slam the door on my foot when I followed her into the apartment. There was a lot of sun coming in at the time, and the fun we were having on the futon raised dust that I watched afterwards as it rose and fell in lazy currents of air. She chose that moment to tell me she was a Christian. She wanted to know if I was, and I've been running a database of lies ever since. As a Christian she did not agree with premarital sex, although minutes before she seemed to find it very agreeable. I asked her what she thought about what we had done. That wasn't sex to her, because I had used a condom. In Hannah's world there were many wonderful things we could do that were not sex. She gave me everything I asked for, but she knew better than to ask anything of me. Three days dry. She wouldn't have to know, in case I didn't make it, but it was something I could do for her. Three days dry in the middle of the wilderness, no bars, no liquor stores, no boozy buddies to trip me up. How hard could it be for a social drinker like me?

Luke holds the flashlight steady while I strike another match from our only matchbook, which may or may not have been damp at some point. I can't even get a spark. The newspaper core, smaller twigs and then bigger ones—it's all ready if I could just light one match. It's getting darker, and Luke points out a fire on the south side of the lake. We hear the faint sounds of singing and watch their fire grow rapidly, not that it's a competition. I'm down to the last match and in the ultimate act of cowardice, I give it to Luke, so he can take responsibility for us being cold, for us being bled dry by a black cloud of mini-vampire insects. I slump back, too wrecked to do anything but swat the occasional mosquito. The probability of lighting the last match when all the others had failed was quite low. After ensuring that we are completely crushed and depressed, Levi goes to his tent, gets his lighter, and lights the fire.

—Ta da!

—Thank you, Levi, for your gift of fire.

As soon as the fire is strong enough to support bigger pieces, I start throwing everything on it. We need a bonfire, the biggest one these boys have ever seen. I want the south-side campers to see it. I want Camp Kahanisota to see it. I want everyone within a hundred miles to see it. Dead pine branches flare up and crackle as I drag over fallen tree branches, then entire trees. It's time to run around the fire and howl at the moon, dizzy, woozy, elated, insane. Fire, the great uniter, brings together boys of all ages. I strip moss off the forest floor and we make awful green wigs, wigs that live, still crawling with life. The mosquitoes can't get you if you stand in the smoke. The mosquitoes can't get you if you stand in the fire. They can't take the heat. When we are exhausted and our voices have dropped an octave from the howling and screaming, it's time for sleep. We leave the bonfire burning and head for our tents.

Fuck you, Smokey the Bear!

Luke and I lie still, the bonfire strong enough to light up the inside of the tent. He wants to talk. Oh, shit. Evasive manoeuvres: duck, deny, delineate! Ask me anything you want about the NFL, but please, Jesus, nothing else, nothing weird, nothing personal.

—Are you shaking?

—Yeah, a little. It's just being away from the fire.

And it hasn't even started.

—My mom says the earth is six thousand years old.

—Go on.

—Dad says it isn't, but that's supposed to be our little secret. What do you think?

—Your dad and mom are the ones who teach . . . um, sometimes there can be differences but those differences don't have to be the end, they don't have to divide, they can just be for more . . . they can be the basis for more discussion. There are different ways to look at things like this, and there is the literal way, and that makes things a lot easier if you can look at the Bible and see it as an instruction manual for life, rather than some mystical, loosey-goosey, vague pile of suggestions that you have to pump through the filter of historical context, not unlike . . . not unlike what you might have to do with any historical text. Does that help?

—I don't really understand what you said.

—Luke, you're a smart kid. If you want to figure out who's right, just look at the probabilities.

All night I shake and listen to my heart pound while loons go crazy on the lake. I finally fall asleep as the sun comes up. Luke wakes me midmorning to tell me the Rebels are gone. The south-side campers have also taken off. I pace, waiting for the boys to return, wondering if there's some way I can leave them here that could be explained. My cells are exploding, and the Rebels are off on a fucking field trip. The knot Luke tied that runs from the tent fly to the tree looks neat, proper, and impossible to untie. I consider "untying" it with a knife, tugging at the loose end like a chimp, when Levi comes up right behind me, scaring me.

—Did you know you tied your fly to a rotten tree? It could have fallen over in the night and squashed you like a bug.

—It's not rotten. It's just old.

Levi leans on it and it falls over, destroying the camp stove.

—Okay. I'll give you that one. That was a rotten tree.

Time to go. I convince the boys that we can leave our tents and sleeping bags on-site and they'll send a boat to pick up our stuff. I don't even know if the camp has a boat. I pull the paddles from under our tent and hand them to the boys as I stumble toward the canoes. Luke would rather point out weird clouds than get in the canoe.

—Those clouds seem atypical for this area.

—Yeah, yeah, yeah, Luke. Let's just get home.

Three hours later, I glance back to see how far we've come and spot a dark patch spreading on the water behind us.

—Hey Luke, does that look like atypical wind for this area?

He silently watches as the dark patch reaches toward us. The wind is an animal, touching down briefly in one spot before springing off to the next. The Rebels still have time to put on their life vests, to listen to me as I scream at them and point behind us. No, too cool or too dumb, they wait while Luke counts down the time until we're in it. One minute, thirty seconds, ten, nine, eight. They're broadside to the wind when it hits, rolling them slightly. Levi finally reaches for his vest but the wind blows it out of his hand. He gets up and uses his paddle to reach the jacket, close but not quite there. On his second attempt he capsizes the canoe.

This is the critical point where tiny mistakes join to make a disaster, from the inexperienced leader and his inability to enforce life-vest usage, to the lack of a weather radio or other forecast information, the lack of camping gear that might have made good ballast, the compromised physical and mental condition of the leader, the lack of nearby boaters, the lack of road access to the far side of the lake, the failure of the leader to teach standard procedures in case of capsize, and most importantly, the lack of alcohol. Levi starts swimming toward his life vest, which has now become life itself to him. Right away he's doing everything wrong: leaving the canoe, exhausting himself swimming after something he'll never catch.

Luke turns around to look at me, clearly expecting something as small, sharp waves form on the lake. I slump in the back and spend a few indulgent seconds feeling sorry for myself. First, get a hold of that other canoe. We're lucky it's half-filled with water, because they move fast in the wind when they're empty. Then we tie them together at the middle crosspiece, doing figure eights with every piece of rope we can find, including our shoelaces. Next we drag Mark's skinny butt aboard and put him to work right away bailing out his canoe with a pot. I get Luke to keep his finger pointed at Levi so we don't lose him, a real possibility as he continues to chase his life vest like an idiot. Even with two of us bailing, it takes much too long to empty the canoe. The waves are about one foot high and growing fast, great conditions for losing a small, bobbing head. I have to glance at Luke's pointing finger several times to locate Levi as he gets farther away. Eventually we catch up to him, then his life vest, which he now wears without hesitation. Someone may have learned a lesson. I pause for a moment to celebrate a successful rescue, alarmed by the sounds coming from my liver as it disintegrates.

It's a frightening wind that snaps pine trees, dead and living, and blows the crests off whitecaps, but at least it's blowing in the right direction. No one can deny how hard this sucks but we're ten times better than ten minutes ago, except for the sea serpents. Attracted by the noise perhaps, or Levi thrashing in the water, four or five sea serpents trail us, not too aggressive for now, perhaps balancing potential tastiness against the fight we might have in us. No one wants to work too hard for dinner. Predictably, they dive whenever I turn around, but I feel them, one close enough to warm my neck with its breath. If I keep my head forward and look out of the corner of my eye, I can see them surface.

We are working as a team finally, paddling our guts out, but I don't think we'll make it. The waves are big enough that the canoes lurch forward and surf on them, great fun if you aren't already scared shitless. I close my eyes and when I open them, the lake is red. I know it's not blood, the obvious choice. There's something about the way it foams that seems very familiar. I dip my finger in and taste it. Wine! Kowpers Lake is filled with subpar Pinot. Keep your loaves, keep your fishes; water into wine is the important one. The kids don't seem to notice, no doubt in shock, or terrified into tunnel vision, or ignoring any information that does not fit with what they know. It's time for a reality check. Luke and Mark aren't willing to admit that Levi has snake eyes. It's not a judgement of Levi, I just want everyone to admit it. Luke won't even support me on the serpent thing.

—The probability of a giant sea serpent living in a lake like this is very low. There is no possible food source in this lake that could sustain an animal that size.

—What about a food source *on* the lake? Did you think about that?

Waves build and wine stains my paddle. The kids may be delusional, but as long as they keep paddling, I don't care. Their plan may be to sacrifice me to the serpents. One good crack from a paddle and I'd be marinating in the wake. It could never be as simple as being impaled on six-inch teeth and sent down a long digestive tunnel. They will each want a piece of me. While I wait for the boys to attack, we sail across the surface of a giant wineglass where six feet under there is death, and twelve feet under there is death, layer on layer of death going right to the bottom. We are floating on top of it. Parents paid to have their children float on the surface of death. My heart drums against my rib cage, not in response to our current drama, but just because it wants to. My lungs struggle to suck in enough wine-scented air to keep the damn thing going. Tremors are hidden well enough in the constant motion of paddling.

I cup my hands and scoop out some wine. Levi is watching as I drop my face in it and guzzle. I haven't felt the breath of a serpent for quite a while now. They may have left us. And the wind is not quite as strong. And is that the camp I see ahead, finally standing out from the shoreline? No, that's a ridge, not the camp. No, the wind was just taking a breath. And the serpents have scattered, but why? Could it be that a much bigger threat is coming? Could it be that the mother of all serpents is coming, hard to see at first but now clear in the distance, a leisurely pursuit for this monster with at least a hundred feet between the humps?

—We're being chased by a giant sea serpent. THAT MEANS PADDLE FASTER, KIDS!

Perhaps I've hit the right tone of panic, because they're all pulling for shore now as we surge ahead on three-foot waves, both canoes straining against the lashing that binds them. There's no point in checking for the mother behind us. Either she'll catch us or she won't. No point in looking, not even once. It would be best, though, if she were big enough to swallow both canoes in one bite. We're close to the camp now, but it looks like the landing might be complicated. Waves reach as far as the embankment, leaving no safe area to land. We're coming in, not much of a choice there. The waves slam the bow ends of our homemade catamaran into the bank, and then we're out in the surf and all I can think about is the bow pinning one of the kids. I grab hold of each kid and heave them onto the lawn. I hear Luke asking about the canoes, but I'm already walking toward the parking lot to find that canteen in my truck. Under the driver's seat, of course, my shaking fingers working the cap loose. Oh yes, oh Jesus, oh God, it enters me, I enter it, into every cell.

I find Hannah in the main lodge, sitting in a big chair overlooking the lake. I sit next to her and look out on killer waves that seem flat from here. I guess you had to be there. The wind is already dying, but toppled trees and blown-over tables are proof that we were in the shit.

—People were talking about your landing. Someone said that when you heaved those kids onto the bank it looked like they were spit out of Jonah's whale.

—Yeah, Jonah, what a guy. Someone didn't pack us any food.

—We had plenty. In fact, we had two of everything.

—You were the south-side campers?

—Yeah, you were the howling demons?

The stern camp director stands behind us with the look of a man of authority whose expectations are not being met. A small knot of concerned parents seems to be worked up, looking over at me with narrowed eyes, as if to stoke their rage. Sea serpents are nothing compared to angry parents. I take another drink from the canteen. I would trade everything for you. I would kill for you. How could I ever leave you? The director will soon attempt something gently hostile, screaming a message without raising his voice, or throwing me out without touching me. I reach out for Hannah's hand and she smiles. I think about all the times we did not have sex because I had a condom on.

—I have a database of lies. But it would be good if you didn't leave.

I don't know if her white light cancels my black ooze. We could have a long discussion about who deserves what and who is worthy of whom, but when you're dying of thirst, you don't ask if you deserve that glass of water; you just grab it. I was a useful person before I was this. I have a job and there are still some people I call friends. There are few things I do well, but I've canoed before.

Oscar Martens has been writing stories and poems since
George Michael carelessly whispered. He lives with his
wife in Burnaby, BC.

I'm grateful to the editors who published many of these stories in slightly different forms.

"No Call Too Small"
            published in *Grain*, 39:4

"The Schadenfreude Rail"
            published in *The Antigonish Review*, No. 170
            submitted to The Journey Prize by editor

"Behaviour Befitting a Young Man"
            published in *Prairie Fire*, Volume 25, No. 3

"Breaking on the Wheel"
            published in *Queen's Quarterly*, Volume 114, No. 3
            published in *The Journey Prize Stories 20: The Best of Canada's New Writers*

"Capture and Release"
            published in *The Chariton Review*, Volume 31, No. 2

"How Beautiful, How Moving"
            published in *Descant*, No. 130
            submitted to The Journey Prize by editor

"The Janitor"
            published in *The Malahat Review*, No. 150
            submitted to the National Magazine Awards by editor

"I See a Man"
            published in *Event*, Volume 40, No. 3

"Killers Are Useful"
            published in *Event*, Volume 37, No. 3

"Lake Pinot"
            published in *Prairie Fire*, Volume 29, No. 4
            submitted to the National Magazine Awards by editor
            submitted to the Western Magazine Awards by editor

INTO CAPTIVITY THEY WILL GO

Noah Milligan

Fiction - 978-1-77168-177-3

Set in rural Oklahoma, *Into Captivity They Will Go* tells the story of Caleb Gunter, a boy whose mother has convinced him he is the second coming of Jesus Christ and that together they are destined to lead the chosen into the Kingdom of Heaven. Believing the Seven Seals detailed in Revelation have been opened, he and his mother flee their home to join a tongue-speaking evangelical church and to prepare for the end of the world, but after tragedy ensues, Caleb must rebuild his life without the only support he has ever known—his mother and the church.

"Deeply moving, sad and haunting, *Into Captivity They Will Go* reminds me of Salinger when he was at his most interesting; it is an intense and propulsive novel exploring what it means to be alive and spiritual in a world ignoring such ideas. I loved its rich imagery, its crystal-clear prose, and its strangeness." Brandon Hobson, National Book Award Finalist and author of *Where the Dead Sit Talking*

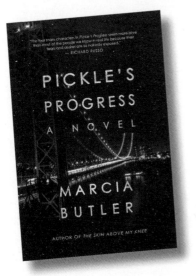

PICKLE'S PROGRESS

Marcia Butler

Fiction - 978-1-77168-154-4

Marcia Butler's debut novel, *Pickle's Progress*, is a fierce, mordant New York story about the twisted path to love.

Over the course of five weeks, identical twin brothers, one wife, a dog, and a bereaved young woman collide with each other to comical and sometimes horrifying effect. Everything is questioned and tested as they jockey for position and try to maintain the status quo. Love is the poison, the antidote, the devil and, ultimately, the hero.

"The four main characters in Pickle's Progress seem more alive than most of the people we know in real life because their fears and desires are so nakedly exposed. That's because their creator, Marcia Butler, possesses truly scary X-ray vision and intelligence to match." Richard Russo

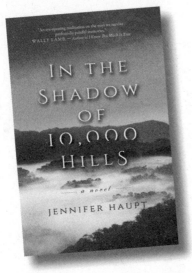

IN THE SHADOW OF 10,000 HILLS

Jennifer Haupt

Fiction - 978-1-77168-133-9

In 1968, a disillusioned Lillian Carlson left Atlanta after the assassination of Martin Luther King. She found meaning in the hearts of orphaned African children and cobbled together her own small orphanage in Rwanda.

Three decades later, in New York City, Rachel Shepherd embarks on a journey to find the father who abandoned her as a young child, determined to solve the enigma of Henry Shepherd, a now-famous photographer.

Set against the backdrop of a country trying to heal after a devastating civil war, follow the intertwining stories of three women who discover something unexpected: grace when there can be no forgiveness.

"*In the Shadow of 10,000 Hills* is both an evocative page-turner and an eye-opening meditation on the ways we survive profoundly painful memories and negotiate the complexities of love. I was deeply moved by this story." Wally Lamb, author of *I Know This Much Is True*